Not waiting for his reply, Jenny crusaded past him.

He clamped a hand on her shoulder and spun her around. "Be honest, Jen," he said, his eyes assessing her from head to toe. "You wanted that kiss to happen as much as I did."

Her chin lifted a haughty notch. "If you believe that, you're really dreaming."

He stared at her in exasperation, feeling as if he was dealing with a stranger, not the sweet loving woman who had just kissed him with all her heart. "Jenny—"

Jenny's expression became even more forbidding. "Do us both a favor, Chaz. That kiss just now? Forget it ever happened."

ABOUT THE AUTHOR

Cathy Gillen Thacker is a full-time novelist who once taught piano to children. Born and raised in Ohio, she attended Miami University. After moving cross-country several times, she settled in Texas with her husband and three children.

Books by Cathy Gillen Thacker

HARLEQUIN AMERICAN ROMANCE

Cathy Gillen Thacker

JENNY AND THE FORTUNE HUNTER

Harlequin Books

TORONTO • NEW YORK • LONDON
AMSTERDAM • PARIS • SYDNEY • HAMBURG
STOCKHOLM • ATHENS • TOKYO • MILAN
MADRID • WARSAW • BUDAPEST • AUCKLAND

ISBN 0-373-16540-4

JENNY AND THE FORTUNE HUNTER

Copyright © 1994 by Cathy Gillen Thacker

Prologue

The samples were good. But they weren't enough, Dr. Lillian McCarry realized as she carefully transferred the precious proof of her astonishing success to a small stainless steel container and locked it up in the lab safe. She needed more corings, along with complete geographical surveys, to prove this was not a fluke she had uncovered, but a well-documented, high-tech way of identifying a potential source. Once she had that, she would be wealthier than she had ever dreamed. Famous, too, because she would insist the scientific process she had invented carry her name.

Lillian shrugged out of her lab coat and turned off the fluorescent laboratory lights. Getting the proof she needed was not going to be easy. But it would be a darn sight easier than acquiring the actual properties was going to be.

If only Gary were alive, she thought wistfully as she stepped outside into the cool still darkness of the

Atlanta night, he could have smoothed the way, covering their tracks and distracting everyone. At least until the time for the unveiling was right. But he wasn't alive, Lillian reminded herself. The success of their venture was now up to her.

And no one—no one, Lillian vowed silently—was going to get in the way of her achieving the dream she had worked on for the past ten years.

Not even Gary's rich heiress wife, Jenny.

Chapter One

"I knew this was a mistake." Jenny Olson shoved back her chair, tossed her golden blond hair and got up in a huff. She had no time to waste if she was ever going to get her ten million dollars back.

"Whoa. Whoa!" Chaz Lovgren caught her wrist before she could exit the softly lit Dallas restaurant. "Don't hightail it out of here before we can even finish our conversation! You came to the right person." He tugged her back to the table, and held her there when she still showed signs of bolting. "If anyone can get you in shape for an expedition into a remote section of the Rocky Mountains, I can."

Jenny tapped one foot, narrowed her chocolate brown gaze at him and pursed her delectable bow-shaped lips.

"But you don't think I can do it, do you?" she guessed, not about to tell him the real reason behind her trek. "You think I'm crazy to even try!" Because I'm ten pounds overweight and slightly out of shape, she challenged silently.

Chaz tossed her a placating grin as he tugged her another half foot closer, looking every bit the rugged adventurer he was in a rumpled blue oxford cloth shirt and equally wrinkled khaki slacks. As a concession to the strict dress code of the Dallas restaurant where Jenny had suggested they meet, he had slipped on the complimentary navy blazer the maître d' had handed him upon his arrival, but hadn't tied the matching plain blue necktie. Instead, it hung on either side of his unbuttoned collar, the twin ribbons of silk bringing out the blue of his incredible sea blue eyes, and the deep tan of his skin. It looked as if it had been forever since he'd had a haircut, she thought, looking over the sun-streaked layers of his chestnut brown hair, but only hours since he'd showered and shaved.

"Now, Jenny," he drawled in rebuke, "I didn't say you were crazy."

"Yes, but you thought it." Jenny reluctantly resumed her seat opposite him only because she didn't know whom else to go to on such short notice. Although she hadn't told Chaz this yet, on the gut assumption he would flatly refuse her if she came out and asked, she needed someone to act as her guide in the mountains. She was secretly hoping to talk him into helping her, sometime in the next three days.

"Okay, I admit I have my reservations about your plan," Chaz said. In his place, who wouldn't have?

Not that Jenny wasn't an extremely capable woman, but she was also used to a very pampered life-style, thanks to the multimillion-dollar trust fund her wealthy parents had set up for her at birth. He doubted she would like being in the wilderness, even for a couple of days. For one thing, there would be no place to conveniently wash the mane of thick shoulder-length golden blond hair that fell to her shoulders in a straight glossy line. No place to wear her clinging black jersey Ralph Lauren dress or the single strand of real pearls that nestled between the fullness of her breasts . . .

Not that she wasn't nice to look at, despite the excess weight she was carrying around, Chaz admitted. Her five-foot-seven frame was very curvaceous. Her cheekbones were high, the features of her face aristocratic and model-perfect from the tip of her straight, slender nose to the delicately feminine shape of her oval face. Unfortunately, despite her traffic-stopping good looks, the most outdoorsy thing about Jenny was the pale golden freckles on her soft ivory skin. He doubted she could race-walk a few miles without feeling it the next day.

And this didn't even take into account the thin mountain air. Hell, she'd probably sunburn in the Rockies, too. Not to mention whine about the lack of proper rest room facilities on the trail. The poor sucker who guided her into the mountains would probably rue the decision to take her from day one. Chaz was glad he wasn't that sucker.

If she'd asked him, he would have felt compelled to say yes because of his friendship with her late husband—and then either regretted his decision immediately, or made up some excuse not to go. Either option would have left him feeling bad, and probably ruined the barely civil relationship they had. He was glad she had sense enough not to put him on the spot by asking. And yet...tonight there was something definitely different about Jenny, Chaz decided as he regarded her carefully. In all the time he'd known her, he'd never seen her this fired up or grimly determined. He had to wonder why.

He shoved a hand through his hair and sat back in his chair. Like it or not, he figured he owed it to his late friend to find out what was going on with her, because God knows he hadn't done much for Gary's widow thus far. "Okay, Jen, it's truth-or-dare time. What brought this on? Why do you suddenly want to go off into the mountains?" What was she really up to now?

Jenny studied her fluted champagne glass in silence, her fingers tightening around the stem.

"Does it have anything to do with the way Gary died?" Chaz continued, feeling frustrated because she wasn't more forthcoming with her plans. It wasn't like Jenny to be so secretive.

Jenny lifted her chin and regarded him tranquilly. "What could it possibly have to do with that?"

Chaz's gut instinct told him something was up. Her actions were too constrained for there not to be.

"I don't know." He guessed lamely, "Maybe the fact you weren't with him at the time of his accident. Maybe you think if you had been—"

"He had help, Chaz."

How well they all knew that! Prim, pretty Jenny was still trying to live down the gossip. "Nevertheless, it's still getting to you, isn't it?" he probed relentlessly, figuring if she was going to do something this crazy, she ought to at least acknowledge why.

"What?" Jenny lifted her chin and speared him with a challenging glance.

Chaz met her chocolate brown gaze head-on. "The fact Gary was with a pretty, young female geology instructor from Emory University in Atlanta when he died."

Jenny's pretty jaw set intractably. She set her glass down on the table with a thud. "That was explained, Chaz. You know as well as I that they both wanted to see the caves and neither of them could go in alone. They were paired up through the local caving club. It wasn't Lillian McCarry's fault there was a rock slide." Jenny's voice caught then steadied as she stared at him. "She did her best to get Gary out."

"I know that," Chaz said gently. The rescue crews had worked quickly, efficiently, but by the time they had gotten a badly injured Gary to the hospital, it had been too late for the thirty-three-year-old investment banker. He had died before either Chaz or a stunned Jenny could ever reach his side.

"Then why are you bringing this up?" Jenny asked tautly. All she wanted to think about was the money she'd lost and her determination to retrieve it no matter what.

"Because I don't want you going off half-cocked just because you feel you have something to prove," Chaz volleyed back grimly.

As if this were a game, Jenny fumed. "Exactly what do you think I have to prove, Chaz?"

Chaz shrugged. How was he supposed to know what Jenny was thinking? The two of them had never really been friends. Girls like Jenny didn't make friends with guys from the wrong side of the tracks, even after they were grown-up and successful. Girls like Jenny married men from backgrounds similar to their own. The only problem was that Gary's family, blue-blooded though they might have been, had already run through their fortune, so Gary had come to his marriage to Jenny empty-handed. Not that it had mattered much, Chaz reasoned, since Jenny alone already had more money than any one person ever had a right to have.

Since Jenny was still waiting for his answer, Chaz hazarded a guess. "Maybe you want to prove that you can be as adventurous as the next person?"

If only it were that simple, Jenny thought. Instead, her life was a complicated, heartbreaking mess. And all because she had been foolish enough to believe that Gary had loved her as deeply as she had loved him. She had trusted him completely, believing with all her heart in their passionate, romantic love. Against all advice from family and friends, she had trusted in his proven expertise as an investment banker and given him complete control of her ten-million-dollar trust fund. Only to find out months after his death, when it was nearly time for her to receive her yearly living allowance from the considerable profits of the fund, that instead of carefully overseeing her investments, Gary had swindled her out of nearly everything!

Fortunately, some of the investments, crazy as they were, were not completely irreversible. If Jenny acted fast. "Look, Chaz," she said irritably, wishing he weren't suddenly so nosy. "Will you help me get in shape or not?"

"Jenny, I own a men's gym," Chaz reminded her. "Besides the fact there are no women members, Lovgren's Gym is not exactly your kind of place. There are no saunas, no high-tech equipment. No personal fitness trainers. Just racquetball and basketball courts, a locker room and shower."

"I know that."

"So?"

"So, you still know a lot about mountain climbing and—and all that stuff."

He studied her avidly, wondering why she was being so cagey with the details. "What exactly are you planning to do in the mountains? Go on an Outward Bound expedition?" He figured that was the most she could handle, and all things considered, it might actually be good for her in the long run, as she could stand to be a little more physically fit.

"Uh, no." Jenny picked up a triangle of toast and fiddled with the caviar on her plate.

"Then what?"

Again Jenny hesitated and steadfastly avoided his eyes. "Actually, it's a five-mile trek on mule."

"And then what?" Chaz asked, intrigued.

Jenny lifted a shoulder. "I stay in a hunting lodge overnight. Maybe for a couple of nights," she amended. "It depends on how I feel at the time." And what she found. Hopefully, it would be something that would explain Gary's actions, and reassure her that he did love her after all.

Jenny? In a hunting lodge? Chaz was pretty sure she knew next to nothing about guns or game. To his knowledge, the closest she'd ever been to roughing it was battling the crowd at Neiman's during the Christmas holidays. She wouldn't know what to do with herself in the wilderness. *"And pray tell why* would you want to do that?" He made no effort to hide his incredulousness.

Jenny's pretty chin took on a stubborn tilt. She met his blue eyes contentiously. "Because I feel like it, that's why."

It didn't take a genius to figure out there was a lot Jenny wasn't telling him. He told himself it wasn't because of the disparity in their backgrounds. He had knocked that chip off his shoulder a long time ago. No, she just didn't want to confide in him. Well, too bad, 'cause like it or not, she was going to. "This wouldn't have anything to do with your turning thirty, would it?" he probed genially.

Jenny rolled her eyes, as if unable to believe how uncouth he was, and said dryly, "You would bring that up."

"Hey, I've been through it, too," Chaz protested.

He knew how traumatic is was for some people. And Jenny had lost a husband a year ago. For a while, anyway, he knew it had seemed to her that her life was over. Fortunately, in the interim she seemed to have recouped her natural zest for life. In fact, she seemed to have gotten downright revisionist about it.

"Yes, I remember," Jenny retorted wryly. "It was six years ago. You had a One-Step-Closer-To-Death party over at Lovgren's Gym that went on for three days."

Chaz grinned, remembering the festivities almost as well as he recalled Jenny's aghast reaction to them when she'd dropped by with Gary. "Fun, wasn't it?" he drawled.

She rolled her eyes, reminding him that neither she nor Gary had stayed long. "The wildest party I've ever seen."

"Too wild for you?"

Jenny didn't answer. "Back to my, uh, predicament. How long will it take for me to get in reasonably good shape for my trek?"

"At least a month, working out every day." And that's a conservative estimate, he thought.

"A month!" Jenny echoed, horrified. She was going to be out of here in three days max and the trip wasn't *that* difficult!

"Even then you may be pushing it," Chaz continued seriously.

"Thanks for the vote of confidence, coach."

"Look. It's not to say you couldn't be, but at the moment you are not exactly—" Chaz tried to be careful "—athletic, Jenny."

"No, I'm not, am I?" she agreed.

"The trip you've described to me sounds a lot more rigorous than maybe you realize," he warned grimly. He didn't want to see Jenny get hurt, as unfit "weekend warriors" were oft inclined to do.

Jenny sat back in her chair and sent him a resentful look. "I know it will be tough, Chaz, but I'm determined to do it."

"Why?" To his frustration, she still hadn't said.

Because I have to get back control of my life. She glanced up and met his eyes. "A woman has to have some mysteries," she said lightly, giving him a charming smile that didn't quite reach her eyes. "Can't we just leave it at that? And while we're at it, couldn't we shave about, oh . . . say, three and a half weeks . . . off my training schedule?"

"Why?" he teased slyly, hoping to worm a little more information out of her. Maybe if they got to the point where they swapped confidences, he'd be able to tell her about the deal he and Gary had struck about Jenny and Gary investing in his new gym.

He'd put it on hold thus far, out of respect for Jenny's need to grieve her loss, but the time for dilly-dallying was almost over. If he didn't act soon, he'd lose the Dallas property he had his eye on. And without the extra income a second Lovgren's gym would provide, he'd never be able to take that two-month trek into the Amazon next spring. "Too much work for you?" He grinned.

"Don't be silly." Jenny waved a hand airily. "Of course I could work out every day for a month if I wanted to. I just haven't got—I was going to say 'the time,' but I can see from the look on your face you think I should make the time."

Chaz sighed. He could already see Jenny was going to be difficult. She wanted to be fit, she just didn't want to do any of the physical work that would get her there. "It would help you to enjoy your trek into the mountains if you were physically ready for it," he explained.

"Then I'll have to do my best to get ready for it as quickly as possible, won't I?" Jenny sparred back. She knew the trip was going to be rough, but also that she was up for it, if for no other reason than she had to be. "So, how are we going to work this?"

Chaz didn't particularly relish the idea of acting as anyone's personal trainer. On the other hand, if he did her a favor, then she'd owe him one. He shrugged. "It's up to you. There are plenty of aerobic activities to choose from. You mainly need to work on your overall conditioning. We could start with something simple, like walking and yoga."

"That sounds fine, Chaz. But there's one more thing. It's important we do this on the QT. Please don't mention to anyone you're helping me get ready for a mountain trek." Chaz lifted his brow inquiringly. Jenny continued, "I don't really want my family and friends to know about my trip. At least not yet."

"Afraid they won't approve of you running off to seek adventure?" Chaz asked.

Afraid they'll find out what a fool I was with my money. Not that she hadn't been warned. Every one of her family and friends had warned her not to let her new husband handle her money. But she had refused to listen to anyone, and look where her stubborn faith in her husband had gotten her. He might have been handsome, smart, passionate, romantic and well educated, but he hadn't been trustworthy.

"Something like that," Jenny mumbled.

"Fine. We'll do it privately," Chaz said with a careless shrug. What did he care if she had her secrets? All he cared about—all he had ever cared about—was seeing and experiencing firsthand as much of the world as he could. He would help her out for his friend Gary's sake. Ten to one, Jenny would wimp out on him in a matter of days, anyway, and forget all about her idea of taking some crazy trip to Colorado. She'd go back to her charities and her nonstop volunteer work and that would be that. But there was still the matter of his goals. And that was something time spent with Jenny would allow him to pursue. Avidly.

"Want to start tomorrow?" he asked, thinking there was no time like the present to get *his* future wrapped up.

Jenny smiled at him triumphantly. "Tomorrow would be fine."

Chapter Two

"I'm ready when you are," Jenny said.

Chaz paused on the steps of the children's hospital where Jenny volunteered three times a week. He stared at her incredulously as late afternoon sunlight filtered down through the many trees adorning the beautifully maintained grounds, and illuminated the thick blanket of golden hair lying loose and free about her shoulders. "You can't go dressed like that."

"Why not? You said we were just going for a walk in White Rock Lake Park."

"An hour walk."

"So we're going on an hour walk," Jenny retorted impatiently as she shoved the fringe of golden bangs off her forehead. "So what?"

"So," Chaz said heavily, trying not to notice the pink spots of color in her cheeks, or the beleaguered glint in her long-lashed eyes, "that designer dress you're wearing is going to be a little hot, don't you think?''

"Don't be silly." Jenny cast a look at the blue sky overhead. "It's only eighty degrees this afternoon."

Chaz was again glad that he wasn't the one guiding her up a mountainside. "Eighty can feel awfully warm when you're wearing light wool." Not that that was the only problem with the suit, he thought quickly as he sized it up with the expertise of a person who exercised regularly.

He could see why she'd bought it, of course. Expensive and well cut, it looked great on her. The cocoa color brought out the blond of her hair and the chocolate brown of her eyes. But the jacket was fitted closely around her waist, which would hold in the body heat she'd be generating as she moved. And the skirt. God, the skirt. Short and sexy, it fit her rounded hips like a glove. Ten extra pounds or no, she looked fantastic in it. But it also was cut too tight around the knees to allow her long, comfortable strides, which was what she would need for the walk they were going to undertake.

"If I get hot, I'll take off the jacket, okay?" Irritably Jenny looked at her Cartier watch. "Now may we get started please?"

"Sure," Chaz said affably. He didn't care how difficult this prima donna made her first session; he wasn't going to let her spoil the day for either of them. Keeping his mood genial and his eye on the future and the freedom owning two gyms would bring, he unlocked the passenger door to the battered dark green Land Rover he'd had for the past ten years. "Sure you don't want to change your shoes?" he asked.

"Chaz, really, let's just get on with this." She wiggled a shapely ankle, showing off her cocoa-colored Andrea Pfister flats. "My shoes are fine."

"Maybe for volunteer work," Chaz muttered as he circled around the car and climbed behind the wheel.

"I heard that!" Jenny swiveled toward him, her skirt riding up slightly as she moved. "And I'll have you know I walk all day when I work at the hospital. Even so, these shoes are quite comfortable. I'll be fine."

What the hell, Chaz thought, they were her feet. Perhaps this was the only way she'd learn.

Minutes later, they reached the park and got out.

"By the end of the month we'll have you race-walking," Chaz predicted as they started sedately through the trees. "In fact, you'll feel so great you'll want to exercise every day, even after you get back from your Colorado trip."

"Let's hope I don't have to," Jenny muttered beneath her breath.

"If that's the way you feel about exercise, why are you going to Colorado?" Chaz asked.

Jenny gave him a sharp look. "You really don't know?"

"No." Chaz paused, wondering what it was she thought he was in on. "Should I?"

Jenny guessed not. It was highly unlikely Gary had confided in Chaz, any more than he had confided in her. Clearly Gary must have had some reason for squandering all her money the way he had; she just hadn't figured out what it was yet. When she did, Jenny assured herself firmly, she'd feel much better.

Wanting to get the conversation off her trip to Colorado, and the highly personal reasons for it, Jenny asked, "How's your business going these days?"

"Actually, Jen, that's what I want to talk to you about." As they came to a fork in the path, he put his hand lightly to her spine, guiding her to the right. "I've been planning for a long time to open another gym." Chaz dropped his hand as soon as they'd completed the designated turnoff.

Jenny smiled as she blotted the perspiration dampening her brow with the tips of her fingers. "Lovgren's Gym has financed many an adventure for you, hasn't it?"

Chaz nodded. "Two trips around the world. That mountain-climbing expedition in the Himalayas year before last. But if I had another one, I could do and see twice as much."

Jenny fastened her gaze on the multicolored sailboats on the glistening lake ahead of them. "So what's stopping you?"

"To be frank, cash. I tend to spend more than I save," Chaz admitted reluctantly. "The property I'm looking at requires an eighty-thousand-dollar down payment. Before Gary died, he had agreed to loan the money to me.''

"And you want me to follow through on his promises to you," Jenny said grimly as she hurried on down the leaf-strewn path, looking more flushed and uncomfortable than ever.

Chaz nodded, wondering why this was upsetting her so. Generally speaking, people of her financial situation had plenty of investments, most of them very diverse. Overtaking her gradually, he matched his steps to hers, until they were once again perfectly in sync. "That's the general idea, yeah."

Jenny paused, her breasts lifting slightly against the silk of her blouse with every breath she took. "I'm sorry, Chaz, but it's out of the question."

"I'm good for the money, Jen."

And I'm broke, Jenny thought, or as close to it as I care to ever be. "It's just not a good time for me, Chaz," she said as she struggled out of her jacket. Chaz reached over to lend a hand, wondering all the while how in the world it could not be a good time for her. It wasn't as if she had to count pennies, for heaven's sake. The woman had ten million dollars!

"You won't even consider it?" he asked, trying to check his disappointment in her swift refusal to even finish hearing him out.

Jenny let out a soft sigh. Part of her wanted to explain to Chaz why she couldn't help him, but she couldn't do that without explaining that she was almost down to her last dollar and was facing the terrifying prospect of not only losing everything she owned, but also being the focal point of the juiciest gossip Dallas had seen in years. Jenny couldn't bear the shame of everyone finding out what a fool she'd been, trusting Gary the way she had, and that went double where Chaz was concerned. Somehow, she felt, Chaz never would have let Gary take him in as completely as he had taken in her.

She swallowed hard and looked away as they resumed their pace, then discovered they were closer to the end of their walk than she'd thought, for Chaz had brought them back around to the parking lot where they'd started out. "It's just not a good idea to mix business and pleasure," she said finally as they approached his Land Rover. She came to a rather breathless halt beside it.

"That's funny." Chaz jammed his key into the lock, swung open her door and let her climb, exhausted, into the passenger seat. Circling around, he pulled a thermos out from behind his seat, climbed into the driver's seat and poured ice water into a plastic cup. "I wasn't aware the two of us ever did anything that involved pleasure."

Jenny accepted the cup of ice water he handed her and, her eyes on his hurt expression, said tightly, "You know what I mean, Chaz."

Unlike her, Jenny thought, he looked cool, collected, as if his own physicality were completely unchallenged by their arduous spin around the park. She found herself wondering what it would take to leave Chaz sweating and out of breath. Only one image came to mind. But she didn't want to think about Chaz in bed. Any more than she wanted to think about how she was letting him down now. She, perhaps more than anyone, knew how it felt to be on the receiving end of one of her late husband's unkept promises.

"That's it? Just a no without ever hearing me out or seeing the property?"

I haven't got a choice in the matter, Jenny thought. "I'm sorry," she said flatly, leaving it at that. "I can't help you."

Chaz couldn't believe she was so close minded. Yet she didn't mind asking him for a month-long favor without so much as even a hint of compensation. It wasn't as if it would be a bad investment. He had planned to pay her back in full, before the year was out. Before he took another trip. But she didn't know that, because she hadn't let the talk get that far.

Jenny wished suddenly that they weren't so close, wished she wasn't so aware of literally everything about Chaz, from his rugged all-American good looks to the fresh outdoorsy scent of him, to the golden highlights shimmering in his thick chestnut hair. Tall and fit, he had the well-honed body of a man who lived a very physically active life. But it was more than just the shape of his taut, trim body Jenny liked. It was the courage she saw in his eyes, the reckless sense of adventure she saw in his soul. Chaz had everything she lacked, when it came to venturing outside her realm. She needed him to accompany her on her trek, which might not be easy to convince him to do now, considering the way she had just turned him down. Maybe it was time to beat a hasty retreat and take time to figure out how to get him on her side—without telling him any of the details of her current predicament, of course. "Are we about done for the evening?" she asked cautiously.

"With the walking part, yeah." Chaz stretched his broad shoulders restlessly and gave her a look that gave her no clue as to what he was feeling. "We still have the yoga workout to do."

Jenny swore silently. "I suppose that means I'm going to have to go home and change."

He shrugged. "It's up to you, but I've got to tell you. I can't imagine you doing yoga in that dress."

WAS THERE ABSOLUTELY nothing these days that was going to go her way? Lillian McCarry thought. "But you're the one who sold the land to Gary Olson," she pointed out furiously.

"That's right. But I'm not sure his missus wants to sell the property. Leastways not right away. Not until she's seen the hunting lodge for herself, which by the way, she told me she intended to do as soon as possible."

Lillian paused, fear rushing through her in booming waves. She stared at the brash young real estate salesman with the carrot red hair, light blue eyes and an aw-shucks-ma'am manner meant to put clients at ease. Perhaps because of the type of rural land he specialized in, he looked more like a ranch hand than a city salesperson.

"You mean Je—Mrs. Olson knows about the properties?" Lillian said tensely. When had that happened? And how? Gary had assured her he'd covered their tracks with a voluminous paper trail that would take a virtual genius to uncover.

"Just found out about a week or so ago." The young sales agent propped his booted feet up on the edge of his desk and fiddled with his western string tie before pushing his brand-new bone-colored Stetson back on his head another notch. "She seemed mighty surprised, too. Guess that husband of hers, God rest his soul, wasn't too keen on sharing his business deals with her."

"I guess not," Lillian said slowly, stalling for time. This was all news to her. Bad news. She had counted on Jenny continuing to be as disinterested as ever in the specific financial arrangements of her trust fund. Obviously, for whatever reason, this had suddenly changed, which meant she was going to have to work faster than anticipated, if she didn't want to lose everything she had put into this risky but lucrative venture.

The young salesman peered at her curiously. "Say, you know Mrs. Olson?"

"No, I don't," Lillian said shortly, although technically that wasn't quite true. She and Jenny *had* met, in New Mexico. Jenny just hadn't known who

Lillian was, or what her connection really was to Gary, and because of that, and the way Gary had died, Lillian dreaded the time when Jenny would find out. There was no telling how Gary's widow would react, or what conclusions she would draw. Or what those same conclusions would force Jenny to feel about Lillian in a business sense. To think that Jenny might exact some sort of vengeance scared the heck out of Lillian.

Not that she intended to swindle Jenny Olson out of anything. No, she just wanted what Gary had promised her. Once she did get that, Lillian vowed silently, then she'd see Jenny got Gary's fair share. Until then, though, she had to be careful. Gary had said time and again that Jenny was a wonderful woman, but that didn't mean Jenny would enjoy finding out she'd been kept in the dark by her late husband. And his mysterious female friend.

Lillian looked at the young salesman. He might only be twenty-three or twenty-four, but she knew it was to her advantage to get him on her side. "It seems to me you'd want to talk Mrs. Olson into selling the property again," Lillian said casually. "After all, you'd get another commission."

Mouth compressed tightly, he got up to pour himself another cup of coffee. "Yeah, but I'd also feel guilty as all get-out for selling what looks to be a worthless piece of land. And not just once, but twice. Course, I know you might be hoping to someday get it rezoned to commercial property status, so it can be developed into another year-round resort. But with many in this state feeling there's already been way too much development of virgin forest land, that's a helluva risk to be taking. Course, it's your money."

Lillian sighed. She was getting very tired of people putting up roadblocks to her much-deserved success. She walked the length of the small Colorado real estate office, trying hard not to pace. She was anxious to be on her way to the property, where the real work would be done, and the results she desired, gained.

"These days," the cowboy continued with knowledgeable kindness, "no one can afford to be sitting on a worthless piece of land for too long. Particularly when the taxes haven't been paid in some time."

Lillian was stunned by what he had just revealed. She whirled to face him. "You mean—?"

"That's right." He nodded sagely. "Mrs. Olson owes a bundle, not just to the county, but to the state, and so will the next person who's foolhardy enough to buy the tract." He sank back into his chair and peered at her suspiciously, as if wondering what she really was up to. "You don't look like you can afford to get those taxes up-to-date any more than Mrs. Olson can," he said finally.

Lillian swallowed, wondering how close Jenny was to the edge in a financial sense. All she needed was for those properties to fall into other hands, before she had a chance to buy them herself and see her and Gary's plan to fruition! "Did Jenny Olson tell you she was in financial trouble?'' Lillian pressed, hoping she was not.

''Didn't have to,'' the Colorado cowboy answered smugly. ''Otherwise those taxes would've been paid by now.''

He had a point. Lillian suppressed a sigh. She told herself she was helping Jenny by offering to take the land and the unpaid taxes off her hands. ''Look. I'll worry about the taxes.''

''Somebody better—''

''In the meantime, I want you to talk to Mrs. Olson for me. About selling that hunting lodge and the surrounding property.''

The cowboy took his feet off his desk and picked up a paper and pen. Having done his duty and warned her off, he was now prepared to do business. ''And who exactly should I say is inquiring?''

Lillian hedged again. She was used to guarding her privacy, but she didn't want to lie. Nor did she want to reveal her name. ''It's a new Atlanta-based investment company, called Properties, Inc.''

''And you're—?''

''That, I'd rather not say.''

''Why not?''

''I just don't want to say, all right?'' The cowboy cum salesman regarded her curiously. ''Just put out some feelers for me,'' Lillian continued impatiently. ''Find out if she wants to sell the land.''

''And then what?''

"I'll get back in touch with you in another week or so," Lillian promised. When I have all the proof I need, my investors lined up, and my action plan set.

"Okay, I'll ask if she wants to put it on the market. But like I said, I doubt she'll bite, not until she has at least seen the place."

Chapter Three

"Don't lie to me, Jenny," Chaz said the moment he picked her up at her home the next evening. "You're sore as hell."

"I'm a little stiff," she corrected. And if she was, it was all his fault. He had insisted they do hatha-yoga for over an hour the previous night, after they had completed their killer walk.

It had seemed like a good idea at the time. Chaz had assured her the floor exercises would help immensely to tone and condition her all over. This morning, when it had taken Jenny a good fifteen minutes to roll herself out of bed, she'd felt otherwise.

"Stiff, my foot. You can hardly move." He shook his head in silent censure as he watched her limp to his ancient green Land Rover, her movements stiff and jerky. She winced as she eased herself into the passenger seat. "That settles it," he decided grimly. "We're going back to my place."

"And do what?" Jenny asked a little too breathlessly as Chaz leaned across her to fasten her shoulder belt for her.

His face inches from hers, he flashed her a grin.
"Why, to work out the kinks in the Jacuzzi, of
course."

Jenny's heart pounded a little harder than it
should have at his nearness. Despite her decision to
keep Chaz, and indeed all men, at arm's length until
she had straightened out her personal situation, it
was surprisingly easy to imagine the two of them en-
sconced in a tub of warm bubbling water. "What?
No time off for good behavior?" she joked, wishing
her personal situation hadn't necessitated a crash
course in physical fitness.

Chaz sent her a knowing sidelong look as he thrust
the jeep into gear and they took off with a predicta-
ble lurch. "Not if you expect to survive a mountain
trek in Colorado."

"Oh, I'm going to Colorado," Jenny announced
boldly as she inhaled his brisk, outdoorsy scent.
Absolutely nothing was stopping her from getting her
life back on track. Even if she was going to be out of
here far sooner than Chaz currently knew.

"Then you'd better work out," Chaz advised
sternly. "Because traipsing around the mountains
will require every bit of strength and stamina you can
muster."

And then some, Jenny thought soberly, wondering for the thousandth time if she was really up to

such a trip. Though heaven knows she'd worry less about getting lost or running into any rattlesnakes or grizzly bears if she had a man like Chaz along with her.

Short minutes later, Chaz parked in front of a sprawling white brick home in nearby University Park. The large quad-level home looked almost as luxurious as Jenny's home in nearby Highland Park. Jenny turned to Chaz in astonishment. When had this come about? "I didn't know you owned a home," Jenny said, pleased.

"I don't. I'm house-sitting for some friends who are in Europe."

"Oh."

Jenny bit down on her disappointment. She supposed she should've expected that. Chaz was too footloose and fancy-free to ever want to be encumbered with a house. His business was different, she supposed, because it produced the income that allowed him to continue to go adventuring.

Because it was easier, they went into the house through the garage.

"Swimsuits are in the guest room on the second floor. Put one on while I fire up the Jacuzzi." Chaz left her in the cathedral-ceilinged living room while he went off to open up the French doors that led to the terrace.

Jenny stared at the Jacuzzi. It occupied center stage of the terrace and overlooked the backyard.

Surrounded by an abundance of flowering plants, it was just the right size for two people.

Chaz returned, shirtless, to find her standing in the exact place he'd left her. She had made no move to go and find herself a suit. His brow furrowed as he stared back at her. "You do want to wear suits, don't you?"

Despite her efforts to appear cool and collected, Jenny felt herself flush. "Yes. Absolutely. Of course," she said primly, her posture becoming even more exacting.

"Oh. Good."

"I'm sorry," Jenny said at last, aware she was acting like an imbecile. Despite the recessed lights around the Jacuzzi and the soft, soothing music that had switched on at the same time as the lights, there was nothing remotely sexual about this. Chaz was merely doing the expedient thing so she could get on with her conditioning. And since, unbeknownst to Chaz, Jenny still planned to leave in the morning, she had no choice but to go along with his suggestion. She certainly couldn't start out in Colorado as stiff and sore as she was now, or else she'd really be in agony.

Jenny collected herself with effort and was relieved to hear her voice sounded composed. "You said the extra swimsuits were upstairs?"

"Yeah, I'll show you since I have to get mine on, too."

He left her at the door of the guest room, then went down the hall to the master suite.

When she joined him on the deck long moments later, Chaz was already in the tub, covered in opaque bubbles to his chest. Feeling ridiculously like a bride on her wedding night, Jenny unbelted her robe, then waited until his gaze was averted before she slipped unobtrusively into the warm bubbling water opposite him.

"That painful, hmm?" Chaz noted as Jenny tried to get comfortable on the bench.

"Actually," Jenny winced again, "yes."

"Jen, I'm sorry. I never would've pushed you so hard last night had I known—"

Was that concern she saw on his face, or just guilt because he'd inadvertently trained her too hard?

Jenny let herself drift in the bubbling water. To her relief, the warm swirling water was helping a lot. "What is on the agenda for tonight?" she asked lazily, trying hard not to notice how handsome he looked in the soft light, or how deeply tanned his skin was, or how blue his eyes were. She'd thought he looked good in the snug-fitting jeans and rumpled cotton shirts he habitually wore. It was nothing compared to the way he looked in the trim blue racing briefs. All muscle and smooth skin, dusted with light golden brown hair.

"Racquetball. Once your muscles loosen up, that is." He surveyed her steadily, taking in the way she'd done her hair—with a single barrette so it wouldn't get wet, and the way she filled out every inch of the borrowed swimsuit.

"You're still looking pretty tight."

And I feel pretty tense, too. Jen slid a little lower, so the water covered her almost to her collarbone. "Where are we going to play? At your gym?"

Chaz shook his head. "On the court downstairs. It's more private."

Jenny wasn't sure she wanted private, though she supposed here was bound to be less risky than Chaz's gym, where she might run into one of Gary's friends. And then they might ask what the two of them were doing playing racquetball together. Jenny didn't want to have to explain, and she didn't want to lie.

"So how is your business?" Jenny asked.

"Growing. I've got more people wanting memberships than I can handle."

Jenny thought about what he'd asked her, about loaning him money for a second gym, then pushed the thought aside. Even if she wanted to do that—and she wasn't at all sure she did—she couldn't, so she might as well concentrate on her future and the problems she faced in the days ahead. The foremost one being her trip to Colorado.

"Does that mean you're too busy to get away for a few days?"

"I can always get away for short periods on the spur of the moment, and long periods—up to a couple of months—if I do some advance planning. That's one of the things I like about owning my own business." He studied her briefly, his blue eyes drifting over her face with disconcerting slowness. "Why do you ask?"

Jenny shrugged, pretending it was no big deal. "I'm a little uneasy about going into the mountains alone." *And I wondered what you'd charge to be my guide, especially if you knew I was down to my last thousand.*

His sea blue gaze narrowed speculatively. "You're not going on a guided tour?" Again, a surprising amount of concern radiated in his low voice.

"No."

He paused a moment, reached into the bucket beside him and took out a cold can of orange Gatorade. "Want to tell me what you're going to be doing?" he asked as he tossed her a can.

"Not really." Jenny popped open the top of her drink and switched the subject to the first thing that came to mind. "So. How's your love life these days, Chaz? Dating anyone special?"

Chaz choked on the drink he'd been taking and bolted upright. "Not at the moment, no," he said, still sounding a little choked.

So, there was no special someone keeping him here. Jenny knew how much he loved the mountains. He spent half his trips exploring one range or another. She had hoped that he'd consider going with her, perhaps even come right out and volunteer to do so, if for no other reason than he enjoyed being in the mountains as much as she did.

Jenny told herself not to take his reticence personally. After all, she and Chaz didn't really know much about each other. He had always been, to this point, pretty much Gary's friend and not hers. She also knew she was a mystery to him; and for the moment at least, she wanted it that way. But he was an enigma to her, too.

Maybe it was the intimacy of the moment, but suddenly she wanted very much to know why he was still a bachelor at age thirty-six. "Why *haven't* you ever married, Chaz?"

Chaz's face lit up with amusement. "Probably because I'm always off adventuring. And speaking of dating, have you been out with anyone special since..."

Jenny knew he meant to embarrass her the way she had just embarrassed him. "I have but I didn't enjoy it. Does that count?"

His eyes sparkled even more. Jenny was aware they were heading for dangerous territory.

"How come you didn't enjoy it?" he pressed with a mischievous grin.

Because I've found myself worrying repeatedly about what people's ulterior motives are. I wonder if they want to be with me because of who I am or because of the ten million dollars everyone thinks I still have.

Jenny shrugged, the lifting motion of her shoulders inadvertently hiking her breasts out of the water briefly before she slid lower and covered herself with the bubbling water once again. "I don't know," she said diffidently.

Chaz slid closer, so they wouldn't have to talk quite so loudly to be heard. "Did they have bad breath?"

Jenny gaped at him, taken aback by the impudence of his question. "For heaven's sake, Chaz! I don't know! What a question to ask!"

"What do you mean you don't know? Weren't you close enough to tell?"

"Chaz!" Jenny groaned out loud and wished she had never started this.

"Sorry," he shot back lazily. "I just assumed. People usually do kiss good-night."

"Well, they didn't," Jenny rebuked sternly.

"How come? I assume they tried," he persisted, seemingly unable to check his prurient interest or tear his gaze away from the incensed sparkle in her dark brown eyes. "Or at least they must have wanted to. Jen?"

"You're right," Jenny confessed after a moment, bravely confronting his probing gaze. "They've tried to kiss me."

"But—?"

Jenny dropped her gaze. She shouldn't be talking about anything so intimate with him, but what did it really matter? She needed to get this off her chest and she doubted she'd ever see him again after the Colorado trek anyway.

She took a deep, ragged breath and plunged on. "It's just been so long since I kissed someone, Chaz." *I worry it won't be as good as it was with Gary. I worry I won't feel anything. Then I worry I will. And if I do, I'll end up getting swindled again.*

"You get nervous, huh?"

"*Terrified* is the word I think you're looking for," Jenny joked wryly, not above partaking in a little self-effacing humor. "And yes, very."

"So feel the fear and kiss a guy anyway," Chaz advised, his expression suddenly serious.

Jenny stared down at the swirling water. She thought about the way Gary had betrayed her and how much she had trusted him, and how difficult it was going to be for her to trust someone again. Never mind actually make love to them. "I don't think I can," she confessed, very low.

"Sure you can," Chaz disagreed in a soft, persuasive voice. "Life's meant to be enjoyed, Jen. Experienced to the fullest. The man-woman thing's a big part of that."

Jenny's head lifted and she regarded him with a slightly bemused look. "That's easy for you to say," she retorted. "You're different than I am, more gregarious and outgoing with the opposite sex. You've probably kissed a million women."

Chaz shook his head in silent censure. "I'm well travelled, Jen. Not promiscuous. And as for the kissing thing, you're making too much of it, building it up until you're paralyzed with fear. Trust me," he urged gently, wanting to help her if he could. Maybe then she'd want to help him out in turn. "Kissing someone is easy, even after a time-out of a year."

Jenny wished she could believe she would someday be able to love again, as well as get every cent of her trust fund back. And all without anyone ever finding out how her own husband, the one man in the world she had dared love with all her heart and soul had robbed her blind while professing to feel the same. "I wish I could believe that," she said wistfully.

"So believe it," Chaz advised softly, as if life were really that simple. He slid around beside her. The next thing she knew his arms were around her. "You see how easy this is?" he whispered, as he gathered her close, until her breasts rested against the hardness of his chest. His fingers closed expertly around the nape of her neck and drew her face up to his.

The touch of his lips on hers was incredible, so enticing and sensual and male. So incredibly tender and sweet. With a low groan of discovery, he parted her lips. His tongue slipped into her mouth, stroking and tasting. Seconds later, she was melting against him, recklessly, wantonly returning his kiss. Her hands curled into the forest of hair on his chest, then moved up, to spread across his shoulders. He kissed the edges of her mouth, then drank deeply of her once again, and again, until they were both gasping for air and wanting so much more.

Aware of what would happen if she didn't break this off, Jenny pushed away from him. Chaz stared at her, looking as if he wanted to carry her off to his bedroom that instant, strip her bare and make love to her.

Jenny glared at him, unable to believe how swiftly and easily he'd put the moves on her. Was she this easy to take advantage of? Or was Chaz just that good at manipulating and seducing women into his bed? Heaven knows if she hadn't come to her senses, his bed was precisely where they would have ended up. "Smooth, Chaz, very smooth!"

"Wait a minute. You don't think! Jen, there was nothing premeditated about that—"

She gave a short, sardonic laugh. "Right."

"Jenny, God. I—"

Ignoring his attempts to sweet-talk her into calmness, Jenny propelled herself swiftly out of the Jacuzzi and yanked on her robe. "I'm going upstairs to change." Her voice was brittle enough to cut glass.

"Jenny, wait."

"I don't want to hear it, Chaz," she snapped over her shoulder as she retreated. She was afraid if he explained, she just might buy it.

"How long are you going to stay ticked off at me?" Chaz demanded as the two of them headed down the stairs to the enclosed racquetball court behind the garage.

"Probably forever," Jenny said, meaning it. The good thing about anger was, it gave her strength. And since she'd learned to play racquetball when she was in college and been forced to take four semesters of physical education to graduate, there was no need for him to give her any lessons. She went straight to the row of racquets hanging against the far wall and picked out the one best suited to her grip and weight. "Let's get started, shall we?" Still not looking at him, she clutched the hard rubber ball.

His mouth set, Chaz took his place next to her and faced the wall. "Fine with me," he said tightly.

Jenny snapped off a serve. The ball whizzed back at them. Chaz jumped, to avoid being hit by it.

His mouth set even more. "Look, Jenny—"

"I told you before. I do not want to hear it!" Jenny snapped. She had no idea why she was so upset. So what if he'd kissed her? He hadn't tried to carry her off to his bed, no matter how willing she might have looked!

Nothing else embarrassing or distressing was going to happen tonight. Except, she amended to herself silently, she was going to beat the pants off him for ever putting her in the position of kissing him to begin with. Because that *was* his fault. He could have reassured her verbally and left it at that. But he hadn't! He'd actually taken her in his arms, put his lips over hers, and kissed her senseless. And all the while, he was probably plotting to use her and her money, or the money he thought she still had, just as Gary had!

Jenny scowled at the ball she held tightly in her hand.

"Are you going to serve?" Chaz snapped, "or are we just going to stand here all day?"

That did it. Jenny let go with another serve. This one he hit. Fiercely. She lobbed it right back, just as fiercely.

The lead was hers. Then it was his. Then it was hers again. Then his. They played ferociously, until both were panting, exhausted, the sweat running down into their eyes, and it was match point.

"You're overreacting about the kiss," Chaz cut in again grimly, the instant before she was ready to serve. "I didn't know it would . . . get so involved."

"You expect me to believe that?" she retorted in her best ice-maiden voice.

"I didn't!"

She waited, her hand clenched around the hard black rubber ball, not believing him for an instant.

He swallowed hard. His eyes slid away from her, then he said, with apparent difficulty, "I didn't think it would be any different than kissing anyone else!" The surprise was that it had been.

For some reason, the image of Chaz kissing another woman made her all the more furious. The next thing Jenny knew she was powering off another serve, only this one was aimed right at the wall in front of him. The black ball slammed into the

wall, then fired right back. Chaz jumped in time for
it to miss him, but he wasn't fast enough to stop it
with his racquet, and the ball sped past him, into the
wall behind them, where it bounced off at them
again. Only this time it was aimed straight at Jenny.

She got out of the way, but just barely. As they
stared at each other, struggling to regain their breath,
Jenny realized it wasn't just the kiss that had gotten
out of control, but the whole situation. Like it or
not, she was attracted to Chaz. And he was attracted to her. That attraction, when combined with
her current financial crisis and emotional confusion
and vulnerability due to Gary's betrayal, was a dangerous thing. She couldn't risk getting sidetracked
into a love affair, not even a brief one, at this point
in her life. There was simply too much at stake. Her
pride, her home. Her whole life.

"The workout's over," she said flatly.

"Jen—"

"I think we've done quite enough tonight, Chaz."

He moved to bar her way. "Kissing maybe. Talking things through is another matter."

Jen glared at him, seething. Hating the indomita-
ble way he seemed to approach every situation, including their kiss. "Are you through?" she muttered.

"With the kissing," he acknowledged. His look
turned intimate as he amended, his low voice rever-
berating with sensual promise, "For now."

Jenny's breath caught in her throat. Feeling she'd suffocate if she didn't get some air, and soon, she brushed past him without another word.

"Damn it, Jen," Chaz said, sounding suddenly very sad and very tired. He gently touched her arm. "Come on," he coaxed softly, then followed it with an exasperated sigh. "Don't leave feeling like this."

Jenny's spine stiffened even more. Where Chaz touched her, her arm was burning like a house afire. Refusing to look at him for fear if she did he'd be able to sweet-talk her into forgiving him, she said, "I have to. I'm going to Colorado in the morning."

Chaz gaped at her. "You're kidding me, right?"

Jenny propped both fists on her hips. "Do I look like I'm kidding you?"

Chaz swore, using words that would have blistered a nun's ears. "Jen, you can't!" he finished. "You're not nearly ready."

She stepped out of his light, restraining grasp. "Well, ready or not, I'm going."

Chaz followed her to the door. "Who's going to be your guide?"

Jenny paused on the steps. *As if you really care,* she thought, recalling how he had passed on the chance to volunteer his services earlier. No, Chaz didn't want to help her out, he just wanted to sleep with her. Would she never find a man who didn't want to use her?

"I don't know who my guide is going to be," Jenny answered him stiffly. It wasn't just her pride that had been hurt by his blunt attempt to get her into the sack, but her feelings, as well. "Not that I'm all that concerned about it. I'm sure I'll be able to find someone willing to go with me when I get there."

Chaz's mouth tightened into a disapproving line. Jen thought she had never seen him look so fierce as he did at that moment. "Damn it, Jen," he swore heatedly, "you can't go off in the wilderness with a virtual stranger!"

Jenny laughed softly. "Oh, no? Just watch me!"

Chapter Four

"I told you you weren't in shape for this," Chaz drawled early the following afternoon.

Jenny shot him an arch look over her shoulder. "And I told you not to follow me!"

As if I had a choice, Chaz thought grimly. He never would have been able to live with himself if he'd let her run off alone to parts unknown. Jenny was so naive in some respects. What if something happened to her? So here he was, reluctantly along for the ride, and cursing his involvement with her every step of the way.

He never should have gotten into the Jacuzzi with her. Offered her the use of it, yes. But he could have gone into another room and read a book or something until she was through. But no, he'd had to play the gregarious host and do the sociable thing and join her. And that's where the real trouble had started.

He had never expected her to look so voluptuous in the staid powder blue one-piece swimsuit. He had never expected the conversation to turn so intimate, so fast.

Nor had he ever expected that the strong-willed Jenny would feel fear about anything. When she'd talked about her difficulty getting back into life, his heart had gone out to her. He had known, even if she didn't, that she wasn't doing herself any favors cutting herself off from the possibility of a romantic relationship with someone. Kissing her had just been . . . well, it had just been an impulse. At least it had started out that way, Chaz thought. But the kiss had swiftly turned into something infinitely more pleasurable than anything he had ever expected—or experienced. Her lips had been so soft and giving under his. Her body so warm and firm and ripe. The truth of the matter was he had wanted to do a lot more than kiss her as the kiss had progressed . . . and progressed. And Jenny had known it and been furious.

She had no doubt expected that Chaz would never come on to her because he had been her late husband's friend. And the truth was, though he'd found Jenny desirable from day one, he had never intended to come on to her. It had just . . . happened. Though he doubted she would ever believe that. Hell, she probably thought he had lured her into the Jacuzzi on purpose, with seduction uppermost in his mind from the very beginning.... Chaz grinned ruefully.

"What's so funny?"

He immediately turned his gaze away from Jenny, toward the serenity of the snowcapped mountains in the distance, and wiped the smile off his face. "Nothing, really. I was just thinking how ironic life is." All this time he had stayed away from Jenny, the Golden Girl, as though she was the human version of poison ivy. Get too near her, and he'd suffer the consequences. Only to find out now that at least part of him, the very male part, couldn't seem to get close enough. And judging by her continued ice-maiden looks whenever she found him gazing her way, that situation wasn't likely to change.

"It certainly is," Jenny muttered, thinking that lately, more often than not, the joke seemed to be on her. In fact it was highly ironic that she, who had been wealthy all her life, would now be tottering on the brink of total financial insolvency. If Chaz knew, he and everyone else in Dallas would probably laugh themselves sick over her predicament. But he didn't know, she comforted herself sternly, and neither did anyone else, and they wouldn't find out. She had kept her untenable situation secret thus far. She would continue to do so, trek or no trek, Chaz or no Chaz.

She cast a look over her shoulder and found Chaz regarding her with that same lazy stare. Warmth filtered through her. Jenny told herself it was the combination of the sun and too little to eat. "Are you hungry?"

Chaz nodded. "Guess it's about time we broke for lunch." He nodded toward a grassy knoll, over the next ridge of the steep, winding mountain trail. "What do you say we stop up there, Jen?"

"There's fine," Jenny said, telling herself there was no reason for her to feel nervous. Chaz was not going to put the moves on her. He had learned not to do that last night!

"This trip has been pretty rough on you, hasn't it?" Chaz said as they reached the clearing. He rode forward, so his mule was walking even with hers.

If there was anything Jenny hated, it was having her weak areas pointed out to her. "Hey," she corrected briskly, "I haven't once complained all day." Aware she'd been slouching, she made an effort to sit a little taller in the uncomfortably hard western saddle.

"No," Chaz drawled as he reached over to take her reins and bring her mule to a stop, "you've just looked either ghost white or beet red for the past three miles."

They'd only been on the mules for three miles, Jenny thought. And that wasn't really the problem. The problem was it had been an incredibly long day, and it wasn't half over yet. She'd been up before dawn to catch a flight to Denver. When she stepped outside, she'd found Chaz camped beside her house in his battered green Land Rover. With no encouragement, he'd followed her to the airport, then the airlines ticket counter. By the time he'd gotten himself booked onto the same flight and put in the seat next to her on the plane, she had known it was hopeless and stopped fighting his decision to go with her.

She had told herself that this was what she had wanted all along—to have someone she knew, someone experienced in mountain climbing act as her guide—and that she should have felt happy about it. But she didn't. All during the flight to Denver she hadn't been able to stop thinking of that searing, sensual kiss he had given her last night, or how good it had felt to be held in his arms. And she'd kept thinking about it, even as they landed in Denver at eight-thirty that morning, rented a car together and drove another hour and a half west of the city, to Fraser, where they'd outfitted themselves for an overnight camping trip and rented the mules.

Now two hours later, with the sun beating down on her shoulders, her thoughts were still more on Chaz than anything else. Oh, she had always been aware of what an attractive man Chaz was. After all, what woman who still had a heartbeat could not have noticed what a ruggedly handsome individualist Chaz was? But she had never expected to be taken into his arms and kissed with such subtle yet searing intensity. And judging from the stunned look on his face, Chaz hadn't expected it to happen, either.

There, however, the similarities in their reactions ended. Chaz had made no secret last night that he wanted to continue on with the exploration of their surprisingly compatible chemistry, while Jenny had wanted nothing more than to run away from it, and him. She had too much in her life to do right now, to deal with a budding romance! Particularly with one of Gary's old friends...

"Admit it, Jen," Chaz prodded humorously, helping her out of her saddle and onto the ground, "you're already exhausted."

So what if I am? Jenny thought as she clung to Chaz's broad shoulders for balance. So what if I want nothing more than to go back to bed, stay there all day, with the covers pulled over my head? I'm not going to!

Slowly relinquishing her grip on Chaz's sinewy shoulders, more because she felt she ought to than because she wanted to, Jenny focused on the snow-capped mountains in the distance instead of the steepness of the winding trail. As her glance turned to the abundance of budding green foliage on either side of them, she thought about her determination to get her ten million dollars back. "Look, coach," she drawled, trying hard to disguise her shortness of breath and unsure footing as she glided away from Chaz, "I can't help it if the air is a lot thinner than what I'm used to up here." *So I'm a little dizzy and light-headed because of the change in altitude.* "I'll adjust in a day or so." *I hope.*

Chaz regarded her skeptically as he pulled a blanket off his mule. He glanced at his watch, then said with crisp male authority, "If you want, you can take a thirty-minute nap after you eat. I think we've got time. I'll stand guard while you sleep."

Jenny thought about snuggling up on the blanket, the golden sun beating down on her body, Chaz stretched out at her side, gallantly keeping watch over her. The image was almost too disturbing to be borne. She shook her head grimly, hoping the innocent look in her eyes disguised the longing in her thoughts. "No thanks, Chaz. By my calculations we're almost there."

Chaz gave her a terse half smile that didn't begin to reach his eyes. "By my calculations, we've got another four hours left."

Four hours! Jenny groaned. Her thighs, bottom and hips were already so sore she couldn't stand it.

"Come on." Chaz spread the blanket over the grassy knoll and returned to the mule for a knapsack. "Let's have some of that lunch we packed. You're bound to feel better after you eat."

Jenny hoped so. She walked back to her mule to get the thermos of hot, strong coffee. Despite her efforts to appear nonchalant, her motions were stiff and jerky. She felt like a marionette on a string, with a wacko puppeteer. Staggering stiffly over to the blanket where Chaz was already seated comfortably, she asked curiously, "What kind of food did you buy back in Fraser, anyway?" She had been so busy studying her maps and arranging for the mules, she hadn't seen. She hoped it was something mouth-watering.

Chaz unbuckled the clasp on the canvas knapsack. "High-energy food packed with complex carbohydrates."

Jenny frowned. She knew she should have tended to the food and let him arrange to rent the mules, instead of the other way around. "That sounds suspiciously like health food," she groused.

"Three-bean soup, and it was kind of bland. But don't worry. I had them add some curry powder and red pepper," Chaz took a sip. "Yep. It's okay now."

He handed her a thermos filled with soup. Steam shot up from the cup. Jenny held it to her face. The spicy scent alone made her eyes water. She couldn't imagine actually eating the stuff.

She put her cup down, pretending for the moment it was too hot to sample. "What else did you get?"

"Ham and cheese sandwiches."

Now that was more like it, Jenny thought. Chaz tossed her a foil-wrapped package.

"So," Chaz said as he kicked back and they both began to eat their thick, meaty sandwiches, "How many times have you been up to this hunting lodge?"

Jenny busied herself tucking the edge of the lettuce back into her bread. "None, actually." Though she said it as if it were the most natural thing in the world, Jenny was very aware of the ludicrousness of the entire situation.

Chaz blinked and leaned toward her. "Let me get this straight. You own a lodge but you've never been there?"

"That's right," Jenny said stiffly, deciding her sandwich needed more mustard and adding some, before biting into it once again.

Chaz continued downing the hearty soup, then drew a deep breath that further outlined the magnificence of his chest. "Why haven't you ever been up there?" he asked curiously, as if already sensing there was something amiss.

As Jenny chewed, she thought briefly about lying to him to save face, then decided abruptly to tell him the truth, or as much as she was able to. Chances were he would find out some of it anyway if they met up with that realtor who had sold Gary the lodge.

"It was purchased shortly before Gary died. I didn't feel up to going anywhere that first spring and summer, after he died." Hadn't felt like dealing with her family's accountant, who, Jenny recalled, had made repeated attempts to see her, to talk about some "problems" with the disbursement of her trust. Instead, all she had wanted to do was eat and sleep and continue on with her charity work, and she had done all three of those in abundance. Which was why she was now still carrying around those ten extra pounds she couldn't seem to lose.

Aware that Chaz was still waiting for her to go on, Jenny shrugged. "By the time I had worked through most of my grief—" *met with the accountant and woke up to some horrible facts* "—winter snows had made the trails up to the lodge impassable."

Not that she'd actually known about the lodge specifically at that point, Jenny thought. No, it had taken her another five months to unravel the endless holding corporations within holding corporations that Gary had set up to cover his tracks. Obviously her husband hadn't wanted anyone in the bank where he held a vice presidency, or even the Dallas business community at large, to know that he was liquidating all her assets and funneling them into dummy corporations, so he could then dispense the funds as he pleased. If not for the diligent work of her family's accountant, who had taken over for Jenny again upon Gary's death, Jenny might not know even now where all her money was tied up.

Thankfully, though, Jenny had discovered precisely why Gary had been doing all that juggling of funds, and had also managed to get her accountant to promise he would keep the whole mess a secret, even from her family, for the time being. Until Jenny could work something out, or recoup at least some of her losses from her late husband's perplexing foolhardiness.

Chaz's gaze narrowed speculatively as he read between the lines of what Jenny was saying. "So in other words, Jen, it was really Gary who purchased this hunting lodge and not you?"

Seeing no harm in admitting that much, Jenny nodded. "Yes."

Chaz's wintry gaze narrowed even more. "Without telling you about it?"

Damn, but Chaz was figuring this out quickly! Jenny lifted the cup of soup in her hand to her mouth and took a sip unthinkingly. The red-pepper-and-curry-laced bean soup was hotter than a firecracker. With supreme effort, she managed to swallow it anyway. "Gary did a lot of things without telling me," she admitted, albeit a little hoarsely.

Chaz polished off his sandwich and poured himself some more soup. "And you liked it that way?" he asked disbelievingly.

Jenny took a long draft of coffee to quell the burning in her throat, but could do nothing about the stinging of her eyes. "I've never been interested in business per se. I much prefer to spend my time working with people, like the children at the hospital and the adults I've helped learn to read. I didn't really want to know about the new tax laws or the stock market or the pros and cons of municipal bonds versus certificates of deposit. It was just too complicated." Or at least she'd thought so at the time. Now . . . now she knew better.

"Which is where Gary came in?" Chaz guessed, seeming to understand at least how truly mind-boggling it would be for even a talented professional, never mind a disinterested party like Jenny, to run a diverse investment portfolio on a ten-million-dollar trust fund.

Jenny nodded. "Prior to him, my family's accountant managed my trust, yes."

Chaz's gaze drifted lazily over her calf-length split suede skirt, matching vest, white silk shirt, soft leather boots and flat-rimmed hat, before returning with disturbing intentness to her face. "And then?" he prodded.

Jenny sat up a little straighter and worked to keep the defensiveness out of her voice. "When I married Gary, I gave it over to him. He moved the funds to his bank and oversaw the disbursement of them personally, so there was no need for me to employ an accountant any longer."

Chaz frowned and poured them both some more coffee. "That doesn't seem like a good idea to me. With just one person handling the trust, there'd be no effective system of checks and balances."

Tell me about it, Jenny moaned silently, still unable to believe in retrospect she had ever been so gullible. "I thought it would be simpler and more cost-effective to have one less person on the payroll," she said simply, looking deep into Chaz's eyes. *And if I hadn't discovered Gary's treachery, I still would.* "Gary planned to check and double-check anything anyway. It seemed silly to pay someone a six-figure salary to do work Gary was doing for free."

"Even so..." Chaz shook his head and didn't drop his gaze.

"Could we get off this subject?" Jenny asked irritably. She had heard what a fool she had been from her family's accountant over and over during the past few weeks. She didn't need Chaz telling her so, too. "I'm sure he considered the lodge an investment," Jenny said stiffly. She glared at Chaz. "And no, I never second-guessed him or questioned him unduly." *If at all.* "I trusted him to handle our investments." *I loved him that much.* "That was, after all, his business." A business Gary had been very successful in before he'd met her.

Which was why she was sure the local realtor was wrong. This hunting lodge had to be worth something; otherwise Gary wouldn't have used the money from her trust fund to buy it; he was simply too shrewd an investment banker to make a mistake, particularly with her money. And even though all the outward signs pointed to it, she couldn't believe in her heart that she had been used as callously as her accountant believed. Gary had loved her, hadn't he? He couldn't have pretended to care that deeply, couldn't have made love to her so passionately and so tenderly, if there hadn't been something between them!

"Yeah, he was good at what he did, no question about it," Chaz ruminated, then added, "but he still should have shown you this lodge before he bought it."

Amen to that, Jenny thought, watching as Chaz dug down into the knapsack and, seeing that she had finished all of her sandwich and as much of her soup as her still-burning throat and stomach could handle, tossed her a crisp green apple.

She caught it and looked at it glumly. "Is this all we have for dessert?"

"Why?" Chaz asked with a lazy grin as he braced his back against a nearby tree and spread his legs out in front of him. In jeans, boots, a blue-and-white flannel shirt unbuttoned to show the white thermal undershirt beneath, he looked rugged, sexy and very male. "What did you want to have?"

Godiva chocolates with lots of coconut, nuts and brandied cherries, Jenny thought. Even though, considering the ten pounds of extra weight she had gained with the stress of Gary's death and her subsequent financial troubles, that was exactly the kind of food she should be avoiding. She put the thought of the rich and creamy chocolates out of her mind, telling herself that her hips would thank her for her diligence later. "Never mind. This'll be fine."

Chaz's expression gentled at her obvious disappointment. "I'm sorry I didn't bring something special," he said softly. "A cake or something. I just didn't think about it."

Jenny wondered what he had been thinking about as she stared at the sunlight bouncing off his chestnut brown hair. It brought out the burnished gold streaks with tantalizing accuracy. Wind rustled through the aspens, rumpling his hair even more. Watching, mesmerized, as the soft silky strands blew

across his forehead, it was all she could do not to
reach out and brush them back, out of his eyes, to
run her hand down the side of his face.

Finding her thoughts once again becoming too
personal, too much on the man-woman level, Jenny
dropped her eyes to the hardness of his chest, lowered it again and found that even more disconcerting. Clearing her throat, she returned her gaze to his
face, figuring if she had to drown in something, it
may as well be his sea blue eyes. She wondered how
a man who strove to experience life to the fullest
every single day could not yearn for the ultimate in
food, as well. Dessert was the only reason she ate her
meal. "Don't you ever want dessert?" she asked.

His gaze skimmed over her, warming every inch it
touched, and he slanted her an amused glance. "Not
the kind you're thinking of, obviously."

No, Jenny thought, a man as physical as Chaz
wanted his dessert in bed. The sensuous promise in
his low tone set her nerve endings on fire and her
imagination working overtime. It was suddenly all
too easy for Jenny to imagine Chaz in bed...
gloriously naked, strong and sexy. She knew instinc-
tively he'd give his all to his lovemaking, just as he
gave his all to everything else he did.

Startled by the vividness of her unexpectedly sensual thoughts, Jenny sat up quickly. If this was where
it was going to lead, maybe it wasn't such a good idea
to indulge in teasing banter with him. "Uh...what

were we talking about?" Jenny asked, trying like hell to get her thoughts back on track.

Chaz blinked, looking as if he couldn't recall, either. Finally he said, "We were talking about our lack of dessert."

"Before that," she prodded impatiently.

Chaz frowned, recollecting, "The hunting lodge. Speaking of which," he said grimly, glancing at his watch, "we'd better get a move on if we want to reach it before dark."

Chapter Five

"This can't be the place!" Jenny wailed, staring at the small, rectangular log cabin.

"Why the hell not?" Chaz grumbled, stopping both his mule and the third one, which was loaded down with Jenny's five suitcases and cosmetics bag. He'd never seen a woman travel with so much luggage on a camping trip and she hadn't even brought a sleeping bag. They'd had to buy one in Fraser. "It's the first place we've seen in miles."

"It's so—" Jenny sputtered and stopped, unable to go on she was so upset.

"Utilitarian?" Chaz guessed.

"Unfortunately, yes," Jenny agreed vehemently.

She was right, Chaz thought, it wasn't much. Three or four hundred square feet, at most, with small windows on either side of the front door. But there was a sturdy-looking water pump out front and a clear cold stream not too far away. The roof looked fine, as did the walls. The smokestack at the rear of the cabin indicated there was a fireplace within. Staying here overnight could be an adventure Jenny would never forget. And that was what she said she wanted in her life, more hands-on adventure. Though looking at her shell-shocked expression now, he wondered if she was up to it.

Slowly, stiffly, Jenny got down off her mule. She tied him to the post, and half staggered, half limped around the overgrown area that passed as the cabin's front yard. One slender hand absently massaging her hip, she asked, "What's that small building out back?"

Chaz quirked a brow at her, wondering if she was really serious. "Unless I miss my guess, it's an outhouse."

"A . . . what?" She looked confused.

"An outdoor powder room," he supplied.

Jenny groaned and spun around to face him. "Some hunting lodge this turned out to be!"

Chaz shrugged, unsure why she was so upset. What had she been expecting, a four-star retreat with pay-for-view movies in every room? "For serious hunters, it's probably all right," Chaz said.

"But worth two million dollars?" Jenny asked, stunned.

The sum penetrated his brain like a gunshot. Chaz whirled on her. To his distress, Jenny's face looked as white as the snowcapped granite mountains in the distance. "That's how much Gary paid for the place?" he whispered, stunned.

"And the three hundred acres of land it's on," Jenny confirmed.

She looked so distraught he was tempted to take her in his arms. Deciding that wouldn't be wise for a variety of reasons, Chaz hazarded a glance at the sky instead. There wasn't much daylight left. The mountain air, which had bordered on uncomfortably warm in the late afternoon, was now taking on a definite chill. Maybe this was a mistake. For her sake, he hoped so. "What was the address you had written down?" he asked briskly.

"Five Mountain Ridge Trail."

Chaz slipped off his mule, flipped the reins around the branch of the nearest tree and strode over to dust off the numbers above the door. "This is Five, all right."

Jenny moaned, stomped stiffly back to the front of the cabin and plopped down on the front step. Tears ran freely down her face. She buried her face in her palms. Chaz sat beside her. "Disappointed?"

She said nothing in response, simply cried all the harder, the tears sliding damply through her palms and running down her wrists. He dragged her onto his lap and held her against him, the way he would a child. Except that she didn't feel like a child. She was all soft, supple woman. "Come on, Jenny," he soothed, his arms tightening around her protectively, "it's not that bad. I mean, I know it's a lot of money he spent—"

"Here today, gone tomorrow, right, Chaz?"

"But this is mountain real estate," Chaz continued, overriding the bitterness and hurt he heard in her voice. He fastened his eyes on her upturned face and—for her sake—regarded her with as much optimism as he could possibly muster. "If you were ever to develop it," he went on with deliberate cheerfulness, "put in some decent roads, instead of a simple trail, you might eventually be able to get your money back. Or at least most of it."

Jenny rolled her eyes and hurled herself off his lap. She paced in front of him like a madwoman. "That would take years!"

Chaz rose to his feet. "So? You'd still come out all right, in the long run." At least he hoped so. If not, Jenny still had plenty more money where the two million had come from. He recalled Gary once confiding in him that Jenny's trust fund was over ten million. And growing every year.

"That's easy for you to say," she lashed out at him miserably as she wiped the tears from her face. "You don't own this white elephant, lock, stock and barrel." She turned and faced the cabin cantankerously, hands propped on her hips. "Hunting lodge, ha!"

He grinned at her show of temper. That meant she was rebounding already. Jenny was so strong willed, so absolutely set on having her own way, come hell or high water, he had no doubt she'd figure a way out of this mess, even without his help. Of course there was still much that had yet to be explained. Gary had always been reckless, but never stupid.

After a moment Chaz asked curiously, "Is there any particular reason you know why Gary would've bought this place?" *Never mind paid a cool two million for it?*

Jenny shook her head dismally. "No," she answered numbly. With the flat of her hand, she shoved her golden blond hair, which was now covered with a thin coating of dust, off her face. "There's a silver mine on the property but that was declared worthless years ago, before Gary ever bought it." She shook her head uncomprehendingly and released a slow, thoughtful sigh. "Apparently, even when the mine was open, it never really produced anything of value."

"Which still leaves us wondering why Gary purchased it," Chaz said, struggling to recall Gary's pastimes. They had included sailing, caving, racing cars and boats, but never hunting, or even hiking. "Was this lodge his idea of heaven?"

Jenny marched past Chaz, her fists knotted at her sides. "How should I know? He never even told me he had it!" Her eyes averted, she rummaged around in her pocket for the key. She turned the lock and flung open the door.

Inside, the building was even more spartan and unglamorous than it was outside, Chaz noted. Although the room was surprisingly clean and devoid of cobwebs, there was only one bed, an old-fashioned iron bedstead. A table and two chairs completed the furnishings. Chaz groaned inwardly as he realized one of them would have to sleep on the hard wooden floor, and it was no doubt going to be him. "Where's the light switch?" Jenny asked, groping along the walls.

"Same as the bathroom and kitchen," Chaz drawled as he swaggered over to inspect the fireplace, which was filled with several inches of light gray ash. "Doesn't appear to have any."

Jenny sucked in a deep breath. "Well, that settles it," she said emotionally, her mind made up. "We're *not* staying here for the night."

Chaz caught her arm. Part of him loved Jenny's golden-girl glamour. Who else would wear a complete Ralph Lauren ensemble, fresh out of the Polo Shop display window, to ride on the back of a mule? But sometimes she got so caught up in wanting things to be nice, she lacked common sense. "Just where would you have us go?" he demanded quietly.

Jenny thrust her chin up. Her dark brown eyes glowed with a recalcitrant light. "Down the mountain, of course," she volleyed back stiffly.

For once, Chaz made no effort to conceal his exasperation with her. "Right, in the dark. Those mules are exhausted," he pointed out grimly, "and even if they weren't, you are." Releasing her, he went back over to inspect the firewood stacked next to the fireplace. As he hunkered down beside it, he noticed one of the logs was damp on one end. But there was no sign of moisture around the hearth, or on the other logs.

Jenny stomped nearer. The folds of her soft calf-skin skirt brushed his shoulder, inundating him with her soft womanly scent. She had her arms folded tightly at her waist. The action only served to push her full breasts up, and out. "I notice you don't include yourself in that tally?" she said between tightly gritted teeth.

"Me?" Chaz shrugged as he rolled lazily to his feet. Planting his hands on his waist, he towered over her. "I could go another hundred miles," he said, looking down into her grimy, upturned face. "But you look beat, Jenny." So tired, in fact, he was tempted to put her right to bed.

Jenny sent him a smoldering look. "Thanks, heaps."

Chaz grinned. He liked the color that poured into her fair cheeks when she got her ire up. "Why, you're welcome, Miz Jenny," he responded, dragging out each syllable in a heavy Texas accent.

With a frown, she reached up to rub his cheek. "You've got dirt on your face."

"So do you."

Jenny gaped at him, then rushed to the pack mule to get her cosmetics case. Chaz watched her haul it inside with lazy amusement. She slung open the top, checked out her reflection and groaned. Her golden hair was all askew. She had dirt on her face, coffee on her collar and grass stains on the elbows of her blouse. Miraculously, the suede skirt and vest were still intact. "I look awful," she moaned.

Not really, Chaz thought. There was something even more delectable about Jenny mussed up than Jenny fixed up. Something infinitely more approachable...

"You look fine," he reassured her, a comforting hand on her shoulder. "But tired, too."

She turned her head and glanced at him over her shoulder. She lifted her eyebrows. "And you're not?"

Not as tired as I need to be to go to sleep tonight, he thought. Until this moment he hadn't given nearly enough thought as to just how difficult it was going to be to sleep under the same roof as Jenny. Particularly with not so much as a room divider separating them.

He stepped back, away from her. "Look, we're here. I agree with you, the accommodations could be better, but they're not, so let's just make the best of it." His eyes held hers steadily as he searched for her agreement. "We can head out in the morning."

Jenny expelled a small, beleaguered sigh. "I guess you're right," she admitted slowly in a voice that sounded very weary and very fragile.

She straightened and continued to look deep into his eyes. "We stay here for tonight."

Chaz had the sudden image of the two of them in their nightclothes. Blood rushed into his groin. Recalling how it had felt to hold her in his arms, he fought the urge to wrap his arms around her back, pull her close and lower his mouth to hers once again. That couldn't happen!

"Great," he said, turning to the door. "I'll bring in the supplies, build a fire, and then we can see about rustling something up for dinner."

"I want a bath first."

Jenny's demand was both plaintive and direct. He halted midstep and whirled to face her. She had her cosmetics case on the table and was already pulling out bottles and bars of soap. His mouth went dry as he imagined what she planned to do with all those tubes and jars. Surely it couldn't all be face cream. Some of it had to be for her body. A body that seemed to be getting more voluptuous by the moment. "You're kidding, right?"

Jenny waved a shampoo bottle at him and planted her other hand on her hip. "Do I look like I'm kidding?"

"Jenny, there's no bathtub," he explained patiently. Not even a bathroom or a closet!

"So, we'll improvise." She pointed autocratically to the pump out front. "We'll carry in water by the bucket, heat it up, and bathe by hand."

Chaz released a slow breath. They hadn't even built a fire yet, which in itself required gathering kindling and bringing in more of the firewood stacked at the other side of the house. "Do you have any idea how long that would take?"

Jenny blinked. "Well, we'll have to build a fire first," she said slowly.

"And heat the water, bucket by bucket. Face it, Jenny," Chaz said gruffly, his patience and good humor exhausted, "you're going to have to do without a bath until we get back to civilization."

"Like hell I will," Jenny growled. Seeing he wasn't about to budge from his stand, either, she blew out a short breath, tossed her head, and shook her index finger at him. "Look, Chaz, I agree we've both had a hard day but that doesn't mean we have to smell like two mules the rest of the night." She advanced on him, the temper glowing red-hot in her cheeks, and poked her finger midsternum on his chest. "*You* may not care that you're all hot and dirty—*you* probably think it's all part of the ambience of this stupid trip! But I do care how I look, feel and smell! So if you won't help me, you'll just have to excuse me while I go down and bathe in that stream we just passed."

He caught her arm as she attempted to breeze by him, and brought her back around to face him. Damn, but she could be an exasperating woman, he thought, even if she was the prettiest, stubbornest, most strong willed woman he'd ever seen. Their eyes clashed like lightning in the sky. "That stream's like ice," he reminded her.

Jenny struggled unsuccessfully to get free, stopped moving altogether and sent him a withering glance. "Then I'll join the Polar Bears Club." With a delib-

erate economy of motion, she grasped the hand he
had clamped above her elbow and tried, again unsuccessfully, to free herself.

Maintaining his light but steady grip on her, Chaz
backed her up against the wall, next to the door, and
held her there with the pressure of his thighs against
hers. This wasn't how he had pictured their evening,
but he wasn't above getting firm with her if the situation called for it. "If you bathe in that water you
will get sick, Jenny. So forget that idea right now,"
he counseled her flatly, silencing her with a look before she could interrupt. "'Cause there's no way in
hell I'm taking a sick woman out of here on a mule."

Abruptly Jenny's stubborn look faded. She widened her long-lashed eyes appealingly and coaxed
softly, "Can't we compromise? You help me shower.
I'll help you shower."

Chaz remained unmoved by her feminine wiles. He
couldn't say the same about the feel of her body so
close to his. It was doing treacherous things to his
lower half. Things she was about to feel in another
couple of seconds, he thought as he angled his body
away from hers. He kept his arms up on either side
of her to prevent her escape.

"Please, Chaz," she murmured sweetly, batting
her eyelashes at him. "I feel awful. I smell worse."
She tapped his chest with her free hand and smiled at
him beguilingly. "And you do, too."

Chaz had never been moved by the Southern belle
act and he wasn't now, but he could see he was never

going to have another instant's peace unless he gave in to her. Besides, he thought as she shifted her soft, warm body against him restlessly, maybe she was right. Maybe the two of them did need something productive and exhausting to do. With only one bed, and one room, it was shaping up to be a heck of a long night.

"YOU'RE SURE THIS BLANKET is going to stay up?" Jenny asked nervously two hours later.

Chaz crossed his arms over his chest and regarded her smugly. "Chickening out?" he taunted.

Jenny clasped her shampoo bottle and bar of lilac-scented soap to her chest. She didn't know why she was letting him get to her. He was just giving her a hard time because he was ticked off that she'd made him do so much work—build a fire, lug in three buckets of water, and heat them all to boiling. Clearly, all he'd really wanted to do was kick back in front of the fire, eat dinner and go to sleep.

Jenny slipped behind the bathroom they'd created in the center of the room, closest to the fire. "No, I'm not chickening out." She was just nervous about taking her clothes off when she knew he was on the other side of the blanket they had strung from the rafters. The situation made her feel vulnerable, and she hated feeling vulnerable.

"Well, hurry up, would you?" Chaz growled impatiently as he rubbed his hands together briskly. "It's cold on this side."

It was hot where she stood. So hot she could feel
her skin glowing all over. "Turn around first," Jenny
commanded.

"What?"

"You heard me," Jenny ordered impatiently.
"Turn around. I don't want you facing me."

"Why the hell not?"

"Because you can see through this blanket, that's
why the hell not."

"Just silhouettes, that's all."

His voice was reassuringly bored, Jenny thought.
Nevertheless, wanting to take no chance of a repeat
of the kiss they'd shared the previous night in the
Jacuzzi, she reprimanded sternly, "Silhouettes are
more than enough. Now turn around before this
water gets cold and I'll make you heat it all over
again."

Chaz turned around, but not before he sank into
one of the straight-backed chairs and grumbled, "I'd
like to see you try."

No, Jenny thought, *you wouldn't, because I'd
win, Chaz. I may have lost my fortune. I may have
lost my husband. I may even have lost my pride. But
nothing, and I do mean nothing, is keeping me from
having a hot bath. Or the closest thing I can get to
one in this godforsaken hunting lodge.*

Knowing the water was cooling with every second
that passed, Jenny slipped off her shirt and vest. She
kicked off her boots and unfastened her suede split
riding skirt, but she hesitated at her bra and panties.

Able to see that his back was still turned, his long legs stretched out in front of him, she divested herself of both. She dampened a washcloth and rubbed it with soap until a lather built, then began transferring the fragrant bubbles to her skin with long, leisurely strokes.

"You planning to finish anytime in the next century?" Chaz asked lazily.

His low, sexy voice made her jump. She backed into one of the buckets as she did so. Warm water splashed on her feet. Chaz started at the sloshing sound. "Don't turn around," Jenny warned. Her heart was racing as though she'd just finished a six-mile race. Finished soaping her body, she began the laborious process of rinsing off. She dripped more water on the floor than on her body, but finally she was finished. With one of the monogrammed peach towels she'd brought along, she rubbed herself dry and then knotted it securely around her middle. Halfway there, she encouraged herself firmly.

"Now are you done?" Chaz asked.

Jenny grinned at the petulant sound of his voice. "Not quite. I'm going to wash my hair."

There was a second's pause, in which she could almost feel him smiling, and then his low, sexy offer, "Want some help?"

Jenny tried not to grin at the lazy hope she heard in his voice. "No thanks," she rejected his offer dryly, with the poise of a woman who was once more in control of her life and her destiny. "Just stay on your side of the blanket, Chaz."

"I think you said that already," Chaz teased.

Jenny's smile widened at the increasingly flirtatious note in his low voice.

"Then I won't have to say it again," she retorted primly as she lifted one of the buckets of warm water up to the table. If her own life weren't such a mess, the two of them so different, she thought, she'd have a hard time resisting him. But they were different, as different as night and day. Chaz cared only about the adventures he went on two and three times every year. Whereas she wanted financial security, personal stability...all the things she'd taken for granted growing up and now, because of her lax attitude toward her financial affairs, might never have again.

Leaning forward from the waist, she dampened her hair then began working in the shampoo. Moments later, the room was filled with the fragrant scent. Ready to rinse, she bent from the waist, dipping the length of her hair into the water, using her fingers to repeatedly slough water up and over the roots from the peak of her forehead to the nape of her neck and at all points in between. And that was when it happened. A particle of shampoo flicked up into her eye, making it sting unbearably. Jenny groaned in agony. Blindly she groped for the towel she'd set aside to wrap her hair in.

"What?" Chaz asked, alarmed. His feet hit the floor with a soft thud.

"My eye." Jenny groaned again and dabbed blindly at the afflicted area with the corner of the towel. As the terry cloth absorbed the stray suds, the pain abated.

"You okay?" Chaz asked anxiously.

His voice sounded surprisingly near. Too near, Jenny thought. She straightened to see him standing on her side of the blanket. Immediately she was aware of so many things. Her nakedness beneath the thick peach towel. The desire in his eyes. And lower still, the unmistakable signs of his arousal against the fly of his jeans.

One hand clutched the towel tucked between her breasts. Her heart, which had already been beating rapidly, took another flying leap. "I'm fine," she said hoarsely.

"Sure?" Chaz searched her face.

Jenny nodded. The heat of the fire behind her was nothing when compared to the heat of his sweeping gaze. She swallowed around the parched feeling in her throat and tried to act as if she were used to being seen clad only in a towel by a man other than her husband. "Absolutely."

Chaz snapped out of his lethargy and spun around on his heel. "I think I'll take a little walk outside." His voice sounded as strangled as her own.

Aware she was tingling from head to toe, and that there was a peculiar weightless feel in her tummy,

Jenny heaved a sigh of relief. "I think that would be a very good idea," she said softly, firmly. In fact, the sooner she got dressed, the better.

"THIS MEAL WOULD BE perfect if we just had chocolate cake," Jenny said with a sigh, several hours later. Chocolate always made her feel better. Which was, she supposed, why she had been consuming so much of it the past few months. She was confused and upset most of the time about Gary and what he'd done to her.

But tonight her craving for chocolate had little to do with her past, and more to do with her present, and the sense of self-imposed denial she felt, just sitting here with Chaz.

"Too much chocolate's not good for you, Jenny," Chaz remarked lazily. "It's got way too much sugar, caffeine and butter."

"I know," Jenny said. And it had also added ten pounds to her weight. She turned to Chaz, her eyes as amused as her tone was serious. "But eating chocolate also makes me feel better."

Especially when she was feeling as low as she was tonight, Jenny thought. Her feelings seemed to have little to do with the white elephant of a hunting lodge Gary had purchased without her knowledge, and a lot to do with the way Chaz had bolted from the cabin after her bath. As if he had the hounds of hell on his heels. As if he wanted only to escape . . . from her? Was that why Gary had done what he had done, because she made him feel that way, too, as if he had to bolt? Jenny didn't know, and wasn't sure she wanted to know.

"We've still got some apples left. Do you want me to get you one?" Chaz offered.

"No, thanks, I think I'll just have coffee," Jenny said, watching as Chaz got up from the table, crossed the room in three long strides and knelt to stoke the fire. Why, Jenny didn't know. It was hot as a firecracker in there. Had been, ever since he'd disappeared behind the screen.

She had never even tried to look at his silhouette behind the screen, but that hadn't stopped her from hearing him bathe. She didn't even have to close her eyes to recall the soft scrubbing sounds of his washcloth moving over his body or the scraping sound of his razor moving across his skin. And the scents... the room was still filled with the masculine fragrance of his soap, shaving cream and after-shave.

It had been a heady, sensual experience, being so near him when he bathed. Just as it was a heady, sensual experience being with him now, looking at his freshly shampooed hair, still curling damply at the base of his neck. The golden hue of his skin and the blush of summer sun across his nose and cheeks only added to his rugged good looks, as did his blue-and-black-plaid flannel work shirt and snug-fitting jeans.

Jenny rose and carried their empty plates to the bucket of soapy water they'd designated for dishes.

Desperate to get her mind off their aloneness and the long night stretching out ahead of them, she asked what she'd been wanting to bring up all evening.

"While we were gathering tinder for the fire, I saw the silver mine out back," Jenny remarked casually, hoping to broach her plans for tomorrow.

Chaz frowned and took a deep draft of his coffee. "Then you also saw the sign that said Danger, Keep Out."

Jenny had been afraid he would react this way. He was so overprotective where she was concerned. But nothing was going to stop her from discovering the real reason Gary had purchased this property in secret, and since it clearly couldn't be the value of the lodge, then it had to have something to do with the abandoned mine. "What could it hurt if we took a look around?" she asked.

"Plenty, since it's been abandoned for years." With a frown, Chaz poured himself some more coffee. "Stay out of it, Jenny. Too many things could happen."

She scowled back at him. Why did he have to pick now to get bossy again? "You expect me to leave without taking a single peek inside?"

He regarded her grimly. "That's exactly what I expect," he said.

"I have to know—"

"Then hire an expert," Chaz interrupted, holding up a hand to stave off further arguments. "You're not up to this, Jenny. Neither of us are."

Chapter Six

Chaz woke to silence. Glancing up from his sleeping bag on the floor, he noticed Jenny was not only already up, but she'd made her bed. The clothes she'd been wearing last night were gone. In their place were the chaste flannel gown and matching robe she had slept in. He grinned, recalling how sexy she had looked in the virginal white peignoir set. Then he groaned, remembering how the sight of her in that had kept him up more than half the night.

They had another long day ahead of them, too.

He rolled out of the sleeping bag and bounded to his feet. Pulling on his shirt and pants as he went, he moved to one of the windows at the rear of the cabin. A hair ribbon was hanging on the outhouse door handle. Chaz grinned again at Jenny's signal that their outdoor powder room was in use.

Whistling, he stalked out to the pump and hauled some water in. Swiftly he washed his face, shaved again, combed his hair into place and brushed his teeth. He was just about to put coffee on to boil when it occurred to him Jenny had been in the outhouse an awfully long time. He wondered if she was sick, then decided to go see.

"Jenny?" He rapped lightly on the closed door. "You okay in there?" He was met with only silence. Heart rate jumping frantically, Chaz rapped again. "Jenny?" Again, there was no answer. He swung open the door and saw what he'd feared most: she wasn't in there.

Chaz swore between his teeth. Pausing only long enough to grab his flashlight from the cabin, he set out for the abandoned mine. He reached it just as Jenny was emerging from the cavernous pit. She was covered in dust, but all in one piece and otherwise unscathed. He didn't know whether to shout with relief or grab her and shake her until her teeth rattled. He was tempted to do both. "Damn it, Jenny, you could've been hurt!" Chaz snarled, more perturbed than he'd ever been in his life.

She flipped off her flat-brimmed hat and wiped her forehead on the sleeve of her navy blue linen shirt. It was designer, it had to be, as were her weathered blue denim riding skirt, knee-high boots and matching denim jacket. Chaz appreciated how she looked in the finery, even if he hadn't enjoyed lugging up all the suitcases her clothes had been packed in.

She sent him a stormy glare, looking too piqued with what she'd found—or hadn't found, Chaz supposed—in the mine to care one whit about what he'd gone through when he'd discovered her missing. "Well, I wasn't hurt," Jenny retorted, her look both disappointed and exasperated. She strode toward him, then veered slightly to the left as she reached him.

Chaz could have fallen into step beside her and said what was on his mind. Instead, he elected to block her way altogether. He wanted Jenny's complete attention while they had this discussion. He didn't want her looking at the warm morning sun overhead, or inhaling the pine-scented mountain air. He didn't want her noticing the unfurling green leaves on every deciduous tree, or listening to the birds singing sweetly in the trees. "But you might've been hurt," he countered.

Jenny gave him a long, level look that hadn't even the barest hint of apology. "I had to see it for myself," she explained.

"Why?" Chaz was aware he was perilously close to losing his temper.

"Because that's the only way I can figure out this situation," Jenny replied. "Not that there was anything much to see," she continued with a beleaguered sigh. She tapped her flashlight against her thigh restlessly as she reported, "Oh, someone had been down there recently. There were boot prints in the dust and some fresh—at least they looked to be fresh—chisel marks on some of the walls, like someone had been digging out bits and pieces of rock. But

that was all I could tell. There were so many different passageways and turnoffs I was afraid to go
deeper, not without first devising something to mark
my way and avoid getting lost." She smiled at him
and fingered the brim of her hat in her hand.
"Which is where you come in, Chaz. I thought—"

"Forget it," Chaz cut her off, deciding Jenny was
taking her search for adventure too far. "It's too
dangerous."

Jenny's expression was shocked and hurt. "You
won't help me?"

Chaz knew this was the point where he was supposed to feel sorry for her and do what she wanted.
But he also knew someone hadn't just been in the
mine, but in the cabin, too. The ashes in the grate
had been warm, the end of one log wet, from either
dew or rain. His temper soared even higher. "No, I
won't help you out," he returned shortly, appalled at
her lack of common sense, "and neither would anyone else aware of the danger of cave-ins and rock
slides in abandoned mines." He held up an imperi-
ous hand, cutting off her interruption before she
even had a chance to voice it. "If you want to have
it checked out, fine. Do what I told you to last night
and hire experts to do it."

"That'll take weeks to arrange!" Jenny fumed.
And the kind of money I no longer have!

"Then forget it altogether," he advised, just as
curtly.

Jenny stepped back from him. "I can't forget it!" she exploded in frustration. "Not even if I wanted to! Don't you see, Chaz?" She spread her hands wide and implored, "There's got to be something more here than what we've seen. Gary just wouldn't have blown two million dollars on a worthless piece of land in the middle of nowhere."

But, Chaz reflected grimly, it looked like Gary had done just that. "So he made a mistake," Chaz said with a sigh. Caring enough about Jenny to be honest with her even when it hurt, he continued matter-of-factly, "So he bought an old mine with the hopes it would pan out. It's only one investment. You still have the rest of your inheritance, Jenny, so forget this, sell it or do whatever, and go home."

Tears welled in her eyes. She stared at him angrily for several seconds. "I should've known better than to go to you, or to any man, for help!" she said. "Damn you, Gary!" Jenny shouted at the blue sky. She shook her fists at the fluffy white cumulus clouds overhead. "How could you have done this to me?" Without another word, she burst into tears of fury and hurt and dashed off blindly up the mountainside.

His gut tightening, Chaz took off after her. "Jenny, damn it, stop!"

"Go to hell!" She crashed through a thicket, fell to her knees, and scrambled up again. He was right behind her. "And when you get there," she shouted instructions over her shoulder as she jerked off her hat and brandished her flashlight at him like a lethal weapon, "stay!"

Just what I need to start off the morning, Chaz thought as he ducked first the flashlight and then the hat she aimed at his head. A hysterical woman on my hands. "Jenny, stop. Now," he ordered brusquely. "You'll get lost."

"Well, guess what, Chaz? I don't care!"

He caught up with her and hauled her roughly against him. "Well, I do!" It was bad enough he'd had to contend with her disappearing act so early in the morning. He didn't plan to spend half a day chasing her up and down the mountainside, and the rest of it descending it uncomfortably on a mule.

"Who asked you along anyway?" She slammed a fist into his sternum, struggled and kicked out wildly.

She was surprisingly strong, and Chaz clamped both arms around her. When she still struggled, he pushed her up against a nearby aspen tree and prepared to wait out her hysteria and her rage, most of which, he acknowledged grimly, wasn't even directed at him.

"Damn it, Jenny, I said stop it!" he ordered through clenched teeth.

"And I said let me go! I don't want you here if you won't help me!" She hit him again, harder. He pressed his torso against hers, using his weight to hold her against the tree.

He caught both her wrists and held them in front of her. "I am helping you! I followed you halfway across the country, didn't I?"

"Yes, but you won't go with me down into the mine!"

"You're right," he agreed, releasing his hold on her and stepping back slightly. His chest heaved as he said flatly, "I won't help you break your fool neck."

They stared at each other, too caught up in the moment to move. And suddenly Jenny knew. If she didn't do something to break the spell, it was going to happen again. He would kiss her. And she would respond. Only this time they might not stop there. His hands might move from her back to her breast....

Without warning, Jenny had an unexpectedly erotic premonition of the two of them, intimately entwined there on the slopes, and then again later, in the cabin, on the bed. She pushed away from Chaz determinedly. There was simply no way she was going to let this get out of hand. Gary had taken advantage of her very passionate nature and seduced her into trusting him, not just with her heart, but her whole fortune! And look what had happened, she had lost everything! She wasn't going to make the same mistake with Chaz, and let her passionate yearnings cloud her judgment.

None of this was supposed to happen this way, Jenny thought as she agitatedly rubbed the back of her neck and paced back and forth. She was sup-

posed to get her ten million dollars back, achieve
some normalcy in her life and then work into another relationship slowly. She was supposed to start
dating first, not fall for a man with lightning-quick
speed and go right into mating. Oh God, it couldn't
be true, could it? Jenny continued to rub at the back
of her neck, and then started in on her temples, too.
She couldn't be reaching that merry widow stage, the
stage where a once-married woman really needed,
wanted, a man? Could she?

No, that was an old wives' tale, Jenny told herself
firmly, quelling her anxieties. A locker-room myth
for men. She might be a very passionate woman, but
she wasn't stupid. And she would have to be stupid
to let her libido get ahead of her personal agenda,
when so very much, her whole way of life, was at
stake. She would have to be stupid to get involved
with a man like Chaz, who cared more about pur-
suing adventure than building a stable, secure home.

And yet, there was just something about him,
Jenny thought, something elemental that kept her
attraction going. Something that had kept her up
half the night and prodded her out of that cabin before he woke up this morning...

*If I were involved with someone else, this wouldn't
be happening. I wouldn't be thinking of Chaz this
way. I wouldn't have been lying there for over half an
hour this morning, curled up in the bed, content to
just watch him sleep.* And suddenly she knew what
she had to do, for both their sakes. Jenny stopped

rubbing her neck and dropped her hand to her side. She took a deep breath and whirled back to face him, plunging on before she had a chance to change her mind. "Chaz?"

"Yes?" He regarded her warily.

Jenny smiled at him brightly. "Do you remember what we were talking about before we left Texas?" Feeling abruptly nervous again, Jenny crossed her arms tightly over her chest. "About me dating again? Getting more fully back into the swing of things? You know, experiencing life to the fullest."

Chaz nodded stiffly, looking no happier than when she had started her impromptu speech.

"Well, I was wondering," Jenny paused, knowing if this didn't cool things off with her and Chaz, nothing would. "Will you help me?"

Chaz stared at Jenny, stupefied, sure he hadn't heard right. "Help you?" he echoed.

"Meet men I could fall in love with," Jenny said, looking up at him. "In my line of work, I don't meet many men, at least not eligible ones, but you own a gym where a lot of professional men go to work out or relax," she continued with Southern belle sweetness he found immensely grating. "So you know plenty of men, probably even the kind I should be dating—"

"I know damn well what kind of men frequent my gym, Jenny," Chaz interrupted gruffly, then wished for one long, immensely tempting moment that he could do what he wanted and simply haul her into his arms and kiss her until there was no more talk of her dating other men.

"Well?" Jenny continued to watch him quietly. "Will you help me?"

What did she expect? Chaz wondered angrily. That he would get down on his knees and beg her not to do this?

For a moment, Jenny thought Chaz was going to refuse. Then he stuck his hands into the pockets of his jeans and, with his eyes boring into hers with laser intensity, said, almost indifferently, "Sure. Why not?"

Jenny drew a long breath, wondering why she didn't feel more relieved. After all, he hadn't kissed her. He hadn't even argued about her request that he fix her up with someone else. She smiled at him, trying to convey some semblance of pleasure, even if deep inside she couldn't begin to feel a thing, except maybe the gnawing feeling she was making another mistake. A big one. "Great." She smiled again, more broadly, and stuck her hands in her pockets, too.

Chaz fell into step beside her as the two of them started back down the trail. Jenny stared at the mine, wishing she could go in, explore deeper, but knowing Chaz was right, it was too dangerous to go prowling around alone in an abandoned mine. She would just have to wait until she could afford to hire a professional to do it for her.

Beside her, Chaz was still talking about her request. "We'll start as soon as you get back," he promised.

"That'll be great," Jenny said inanely, again.

"Just perfect," Chaz echoed, looking deep into her eyes.

LILLIAN HOOKED THE DRILL up to the portable generator, turned it on and sat back to wait. It would be hours before she was finished. Hours before she knew if what she had found in Colorado would also be found here in Idaho.

She walked back to her pickup truck, climbed into the cab and unscrewed the lid on her thermos of coffee. The simple action brought back a flood of memories. She had done this same thing a half-dozen times, but before there had been a difference. Those other times, Gary had been with her, waiting and watching, sharing the triumphs just as he had shared their defeats.

She closed her eyes, recalling, without wanting to, what a smart, sexy man he had been. If only he hadn't been so devoted to Jenny, the two of them might have had a fling. More than a fling if she'd had her way, Lillian acknowledged silently. She winced, recalling the one time she had offered herself to Gary and he had declined. It wasn't a humiliation she had been willing to suffer again. Nor had he ever mentioned it. But his gentle refusal had remained between them, keeping them apart, even as they got closer to their ultimate goal.

Gary had been devoted to his wife. Extremely so. Everything he had done had been not so much for him, or even for Lillian, but for Jenny. Because he had felt he hadn't given her enough. Lillian wondered what it would feel like to have a man as in love with her as Gary had been with Jenny. She wondered if Jenny knew how lucky she had been, then decided she probably did. Certainly Jenny's grief explained why it had taken her so long to come to grips with her and Gary's financial affairs. Probably she hadn't wanted to deal with it any more than Lillian had wanted to deal with Gary's unshakable allegiance to his wealthy wife. So Jenny had let things slide until there was absolutely no avoiding it any longer. And then she had found out things she probably hadn't wanted to know.

Lillian poured herself a cup of coffee and sipped the hot, steaming liquid and continued to reflect on the past. Her job now would be so much easier if Gary hadn't been so in love with his wife, so determined to bring something to his marriage without subjecting Jenny to any of the worry and stress and strain Lillian was experiencing now. Maybe then she and Gary could have had an open partnership, one Jenny might even have known about. Maybe then she wouldn't be skulking around now, afraid of losing everything she had worked so hard to discover.

Oh, she and Gary still would have had to keep their activities secret, because of the clandestine nature of their business. But she wouldn't have to be running around behind Jenny's back, trying like hell to stay one step ahead of her and to purchase via mortgage the land Gary had already bought outright. She wouldn't be so worried about getting her fair share of the deal. And she wouldn't feel so guilty for all Jenny still didn't know, or worry so much about how Jenny would react when she found out how, and especially with whom, Gary had deceived her.

Chapter Seven

"It'll be good to be home again," Chaz said as they emerged from the taxi in front of the terminal at Denver airport.

"Probably will be for you," Jenny said tersely, waiting to collect her luggage out of the trunk.

The cab driver opened the trunk from the inside, then hustled back to join them. Chaz moved aside to give the man room to work. "What do you mean?"

"I mean," she stated clearly as she lugged two of her suitcases over to the curb, where an airline baggage attendant stood at the ready with a cart, "I'm not going back to Dallas. At least not yet," she amended as Chaz handed the rest of her suitcases over to the attendant. "I'm going to Idaho."

Chaz did a double take. "You're kidding, right?"

"Nope, I'm not." She strode over to the portable baggage desk on the sidewalk and directed the uniformed attendant to take all her luggage into the terminal with her, as she wasn't yet ticketed.

Chaz had known Jenny was still irritated with him for refusing to go down into the abandoned mine with her. She'd barely spoken two words to him the entire way down the mountainside yesterday, and then had barricaded herself in her motel room last night, ordered dinner in, and had almost left without him for the airport this morning. Considering how much money she had lost on the Colorado property, through Gary's ineptness, he even understood her bad mood. Maybe he didn't expect the emotional wall she had erected around her. It was as if, despite all they had shared on this trip, she was telling him he could get so close and no further.

"Why Idaho?" Chaz asked, keeping pace with her as she sashayed through the automatic doors into the terminal and headed for the American Airlines desk.

Jenny took her place at the end of the line, opened her purse and searched through a stack of credit cards. "The same reason I was in Colorado. Because I own property there."

"What kind of property?"

"I'm not sure, actually," she said distractedly. She pursed her lips as she finally pulled out a charge card, closed her clutch case and slipped it back into her purse. "I believe it's a farm."

Her cheeks slightly pink, she took another two steps forward in line. Chaz followed her, staying close to her heels. "Don't tell me," Chaz guessed dryly. "Gary bought that, too?"

"Yes." Chin high, Jenny stared straight ahead. "And now if your curiosity is satisfied, I'd prefer not to discuss this any further."

Chaz lifted his gaze from the mesmerizing sway of her hips in the navy skirt. Was it his imagination or was Jenny beginning to lose a little weight on this trip?

He lengthened his strides and caught up with her in no time. "Wait a minute, Jenny. You can't just run off alone."

"Don't worry, Chaz." She whirled to face him so abruptly that he almost collided with her. "Compared to the last expedition, this trip will be a breeze. I can even drive all the way there from the airport in Boise."

Chaz didn't trust Jenny when she was behaving this impetuously. "How far outside Boise is this farm?" He set down his single carryon and backpack with a thud.

Jenny tossed the softly curling ends of her hair over her shoulder. "What is this?" she asked lightly, not sparing him so much as a glance. "The Spanish Inquisition?"

Seeing it was her turn at the ticket desk, Jenny glided forward gracefully and told the agent she wanted to be booked on the next flight to Boise, which was leaving in thirty minutes. Handing over her credit card, she said, "And I'd like an aisle seat, please."

Holding on to his dwindling patience by a thread, Chaz stepped in line behind her. "You can't just traipse off into the middle of nowhere by yourself," he informed her, not caring that the other passengers around them were beginning to stare.

"Why not?"

"Because something might happen to you."

"Chaz—"

"I'm sorry, Ms. Olson," the airlines attendant put down the phone. "There's a problem with your card. It's been . . . declined."

Jenny's embarrassment was immediate and acute. Her cheeks turned dark pink. She sorted through her cards, and pulled out another. "Try this one," she said to the clerk, then turned to Chaz and murmured in way of explanation. "I probably forgot to pay my bill. I've been so preoccupied lately."

Still, Chaz thought, puzzled, a person like Jenny ought to have plenty of balance left.

Again the clerk called in the request. While they all waited for the result, Jenny sighed and ran a hand through the softness of her hair, pushing it back.

Chaz bent down to speak into her ear. "I meant what I said, Jenny. I don't think you should go off alone. Particularly in a rural area. What if you get stuck in the mud or have a flat tire or your car breaks down?"

"Then I'll do what I always do and call the auto club."

"Assuming of course you could easily get to a phone."

"The place I am going to is not supposed to be that remote."

Supposed to be. Did that mean she knew as little about this property as she had the cabin in Colorado?

"The purchase was approved," the ticket agent said. She handed over a red-and-blue envelope. "Here's your ticket. And we did get you an aisle seat."

"Thanks."

Chaz stepped up to the agent. He didn't have near the credit card power Jenny did, but he had enough to get him to Boise. "Book me on the same flight."

"Chaz." Jenny reached out to take his arm. She looked at him directly, for the first time since they'd entered the terminal. As their gazes meshed, her sable brown eyes softened marginally. "Look, I appreciate your help. It was very generous of you to take the time to come with me as far as Colorado. But your duties as my personal trainer and mountain guide have now ended." She spoke with quiet authority. "You can go home now. Really."

The problem was, Chaz thought, he didn't want to go home. He wanted to stay here with Jenny. And that stunned him. He wasn't in the habit of feeling this responsible for anyone, save himself.

"Please, Chaz," Jenny put her hand over his, before he could give the agent his credit card. "Forget about going on to Boise and go back to Dallas."

Her words were urgent, sincere. They also had a ring of desperation. Jenny wasn't kidding around here, Chaz realized, stunned. She really wanted to get rid of him. Pronto.

Chaz stepped back, not about to let her see how her dismissal stung. So what if she wanted to ditch him? It wasn't as if he hadn't been ditched by a woman before, once he had served his purpose. He had been, and in this particular case, for reasons that were quite understandable. No matter how temporarily enamored they were of his adventuresome lifestyle, women of Jenny's class did not mix—permanently, anyway—with men of his. He knew that. He even thought he had accepted it. And he had, until Jenny had come along, he reflected soberly. Until she had kissed him back as if she meant it. Because not until then had he ever had a taste of what he could have . . .

"What about our agreement?" Chaz asked softly. He had the pleasure of seeing her dark eyes widen from beneath the fringe of thick gold lashes. "I thought I was supposed to help you find your next Mr. Right."

"Oh, that." Caught off guard, Jenny stopped in mid-getaway. Her high heels digging into the floor, she moved the majority of her weight from foot to foot. "We'll do that when I get back," she promised.

Sure we will, Chaz thought. I bet when we get back you won't even want to see me. You just said that before so I wouldn't kiss you again. And the ploy had worked, cooling his ardor as promptly as a bucket of ice water on flames. "When will you get back?" Chaz pressed.

Jenny's look turned vague. She avoided his eyes and concentrated on folding her airline ticket into her purse. "Um, I'm not sure yet."

Yeah, right, Chaz thought. He had the feeling Jenny knew exactly what she was going to do. And when and where. She just hadn't told him yet. Knowing how badly she wanted to get rid of him, he told himself decisively, he should just let her go. But how could he, when he had no idea what she was walking into?

JENNY WAS TEN MILES out of Boise when she noticed the car following her. Twelve miles, when she'd figured out who it was. She pulled over to the side and got out. Damn Chaz Lovgren anyway. Why couldn't he get the message she wanted to be left alone? Wasn't it enough that she had to suffer the humiliation of being broke and desperate without him tagging along to witness her incredibly swift descent into poverty firsthand? "What are you doing here?" she demanded.

"What does it look like I'm doing?" Chaz drawled as he got out to join her.

With the sunlight bringing out the golden streaks in his thick chestnut hair, his handsome face rimmed with the beginnings of his five-o'clock shadow, he had never looked more masculine, or daunting.

"I'm making sure you're okay."

Jenny dragged her eyes from the ruggedly handsome contours of his face and focused on the miles of potato fields on either side of them. "This is ridiculous," she stormed. "You have to stop following me!"

"No," Chaz corrected with a deadpan grin. "Ridiculous is having to rent two cars to do it!"

Jenny had no ready answer for that. Renting two cars was an unnecessary expense if they were both going to the same place. Especially since she'd found out at the car rental place she was now over the limit on two more of her credit cards.

Unwilling to let Chaz see her at a loss, even for a moment, however, Jenny spun around on her heel and stalked back up the road to the rental car. If he wanted to play bodyguard, what did she care? It was his own time he was wasting, not hers. She wasn't going to alter her plans one iota to accommodate him.

And she didn't, not the next half hour or the next, or the next. She stopped when she felt like it, got a cold drink, pumped more gas into her car, used the facilities and headed on out again. Chaz dogged her every move, not speaking to her, yet letting her know he was there, right behind her, every step of the way.

And though he'd done nothing more overt to displease her, in fact had taken pains to stay out of the way and not speak to her directly, Jenny was still livid by the time she reached her property. Maybe because every time she looked back and saw him, she was reminded of the passionate way he had kissed her in the Jacuzzi, the same way he had wanted to kiss her that last morning in the mountains, when he'd found her coming out of the mine...

She had bought herself a reprieve from his advances by asking him to help her find a suitable beau. But that reprieve wasn't likely to last long, Jenny thought as she checked the address on the rural mailbox with the one on the notepad in her hand.

Telling herself she could handle Chaz as well as she could handle whatever Gary had dealt her before he died, she turned her car into the driveway, parked next to the two-story farmhouse, and got stiffly out of the car.

Chaz got lithely out of his, looking none the worse for wear after his long drive. He took off his mirrored aviator sunglasses and slid one stem through the first open buttonhole on his long-sleeve pine green shirt.

"What is this place?" he asked, coming up to join her.

Jenny forced her gaze away from the mesmerizing blue of Chaz's eyes and looked around at the rolling fields of green and the pretty white farmhouse with the dark green shutters that was Americana enough to have been the inspiration for a Norman Rockwell painting. "I guess it's exactly what it looks like, a potato farm," she said, unable to help but feel disappointed.

Chaz blinked. "Gary bought a potato farm?"

Feeling a little bit like Alice in Wonderland, Jenny lifted one of her suitcases along with her vanity case from the car. "Gets curiouser and curiouser, doesn't it?" she asked grimly.

He followed suit, retrieving his two small bags out of his trunk. "Now what are you doing?" she snapped.

"Gee, Jenny," he parried back dryly, with a sly smile. "I don't know."

Jenny refused to notice the soft, curly brown hairs springing out of the open collar of his shirt and faced him down stalwartly. It was obvious she wasn't going to be able to get rid of him. She could, however, handle him. "If you stay here," she warned gruffly, "I expect you to stay out of my way."

"Now *that,* sweetheart, depends on what you plan to do while you're here." He set his bags down, girded his thighs and folded his arms across his powerful chest. "Any more abandoned silver mines you intend to explore?"

"Not a one," Jenny replied smugly, wishing he didn't look so male. This house, so remote . . .

"But there's a catch, isn't there?" Chaz guessed shrewdly, picking up on her unease. "Something you're not telling me?"

Damn, she thought. No one had ever been able to read her so accurately, not even Gary, or her parents. Despite her decision to retain her cool, Jenny's spine stiffened defensively beneath her cashmere sweater. "You have an overactive imagination."

"And you, my darling, have an overactive mind." Chaz took three steps nearer, not stopping until they were nose to nose. "What are you up to, Jenny?" He glared down at her suspiciously.

She looked at him, doing her best to retain an innocent posture. She knew she would sound like a fool if she told him how she had hoped this trip would pan out. Particularly since none of what she'd hoped for had come true in Colorado. "Nothing. Not a gosh darned thing."

"Yeah, right," Chaz said, rolling his eyes.

Their standoff over, for the moment anyway, the two of them headed for the front porch. Using one of the keys she had found in her and Gary's safety deposit box, Jenny unlocked the door and let them in.

"Not bad, if you like early farmhouse," Chaz remarked, looking around at the decor. Every wall was papered in tiny country prints. The drapes were of coordinating fabric, the wood floors polished to a high sheen, the furniture cozy and overstuffed.

Jenny walked through, amazed because she liked the farmhouse so much. "It has a really nice kitchen, too," she said, pausing in the portal of the huge, homey room with the fireplace at one end and the professional-sized cookstove at the other.

"Yeah, it is nice. I wonder what he was thinking when he bought it, though," Chaz said. Jenny gave him a sharp look. "Sorry," Chaz said, setting down his backpack. He moved to stand beside her. "It's just that, his love for weekend adventuring aside, Gary was such a city person. It's hard to figure what he could've been thinking when he bought this place."

Jenny had the same thoughts, but she shrugged nonchalantly. "Maybe the soil is great."

"Maybe," Chaz said, looking as worried as Jenny felt.

Before she could say anything else, footsteps sounded loudly on the porch. "Howdy, neighbor!"

"Hi." Jenny and Chaz spoke in unison as they headed back across the parlor to see a farmer in a straw hat and overalls on the other side of the screen door.

Jenny started to usher him in, but he pointed to his muddy boots, so they joined him on the front porch instead. He introduced himself with a hearty handshake. "Name's Whit O'Connor. I own the place next door. Saw your cars drive in. You folks fixing to stay a while?"

"I'm not sure yet." Jenny smiled. "I'm Jenny Olson, and this is Chaz Lovgren, a friend of mine."

Whit nodded at them. "Pleased to make your acquaintance, folks."

"My late husband bought this farm as an investment," Jenny continued, hoping Whit O'Connor could shed some light on the subject and tell her why.

But Whit only shook his head. "Yep." He removed his hat and scratched his snowy white thatch of hair. "He was a strange one, all right." Whit plopped his hat back on his head. "No offense, ma'am."

"None taken," Jenny said. "What do you mean, he was a strange one?" she asked curiously.

"Well, he paid near twenty-five percent more than what the appraisers tell me this land was worth. Planned to farm himself, he said, then didn't. Ended up leasing out the farmland to me." Whit jammed a thumb in the direction of the fields behind him. "Those're my potatoes you see planted. Since you get a percentage of the crop yield, you'll be glad to know that it looks like they're coming up just fine. In fact, if we have good weather, we'll have a banner year."

"How much money are we talking about?" Jenny asked as she felt her hopes rise. Maybe this was the break she'd been looking for.

"Well, if it's a good year, like I'm expecting, your cut oughta run you a couple thousand dollars," Whit said.

It was all Jenny could do not to groan out loud. A couple thousand dollars was a drop in the bucket when compared to what she'd lost. Still, trying to keep her chin up, she asked as pleasantly as possible, "How are property values now?"

"Not good," Whit admitted with a reluctant grimace. "If you waited for the right buyer to come along, you *might* get market value for it. Not what your husband paid for it, though."

Jenny nodded. She'd lament her loss later, in private. "Thanks."

"Is there anything else you can tell us?" Chaz asked before Whit could go. "Any other plans Gary might have had for this place?"

"Hmm." Whit rubbed his jaw thoughtfully. "There was what he did to the well out back. Tried to expand it. Unfortunately, he never got the job more'n half-done. I guess he intended to have it filled with water he trucked in, which is what everyone else does out here when their wells run dry. He never got around to filling it, though. Or *finishing* it, for that matter."

"Wait a minute," Jenny interrupted, with a raised hand. "You're telling me I have no water here?"

"Just what's in the emergency reservoir next to the farmhouse."

Jenny raced around the side of the porch, to see a big green metal drum roughly one story tall and fifteen feet long. "Which is how much?"

"Couple hundred gallons or so."

"Is it full?"

"I believe so, yes."

Jenny breathed a sigh of relief.

"If you want more than that you're going to have to pay to hook up to the city lines," Whit continued.

"Which will cost how much?" Jenny asked.

"Ten thousand or so, minimum," Whit said affably. "It's quite aways, from here to there."

"Thanks." Jenny smiled at him. She was still furious with Gary, but Whit had been nothing but kind.

"You'll be pleased to know the phone's been turned on, too."

"Phone?" Chaz and Jenny said in unison.

"Yeah. The truck was here, oh, about two weeks ago," Whit said.

"How'd they get in?" Jenny asked, her brow furrowing. To her knowledge, she was the only one who had a key!

"Didn't have to come in. They were able to do whatever they needed to do from the outside," Whit said with another smile.

"Has anyone else been here?" Chaz asked with a perplexed frown.

Whit blinked. "When?"

"In the last week or so."

"Couldn't rightly say. The missus and I went up to Lewiston, to visit her sister. We just got back this morning ourselves. Why do you ask?"

"No reason," Chaz said.

Jenny shot him a sharp, inquiring look from beneath her lashes. No reason, my foot! she thought.

"Well, listen, folks." Whit plopped his hat back onto his head, covering his snowy white hair. "If there's anything I can do for you, anything you need, I'm right next door."

As soon as they'd thanked Whit for his kindness and he had left, Chaz and Jenny walked back inside. "Why did you ask if anyone else had been here?"

Chaz went through the parlor to the kitchen and picked up the phone. He held it to his ear, listening. "It just stands to reason if someone had the phone turned on, that they might have come out here, too."

Jenny had had the same thought. Somehow, it was more frightening hearing Chaz voice it aloud.

Chaz tried the light switch for the overhead light, and saw it come on. He turned to her. "Do you keep the utilities turned on here all the time?"

Jenny shrugged. "I don't know."

"Have you been paying or receiving any bills?"

"No. In fact, under the circumstances, if any bills had come in, I probably would've had the utilities turned off."

"Hmm." Chaz switched the overhead light back off. "Gotten any overdue notices?"

"No."

Chaz pressed the toggle switch on the phone, clearing the line so he could make a call, then quickly dialed four numbers. Jenny watched, fascinated, as he made several quick calls. Finally he replaced the receiver in the cradle.

"Well?" Jenny said, dying to know what his sleuthing had uncovered.

"Ma Bell had a phoned-in request several weeks ago, asking that the phone here at the farm be turned back on. The same thing happened at the power company."

"Who paid the deposits?"

"The same person who made the requests, a Mrs. Gary Olson."

Jenny gasped, unnerved by the fact someone was running around doing things in her name. "But I never—"

"I know." Chaz's eyes met hers. "Nevertheless, both Ma Bell and the power company received money orders, made out in your name, to cover the deposits."

Jenny mulled that over. "Where are they sending the bills?"

"Here. Although the first ones won't come in for another couple of weeks."

Jenny sank into a chair. "This is getting a little scary, Chaz."

"Maybe you should turn the matter over to the police."

"And have the scandal become public? No thanks."

"Jenny—"

"Thus far, Chaz, no real harm has been done. You can see yourself the house is in fine condition. Let's just wait and see what else develops."

Chaz continued to study her in silence. Finally he released a long breath. "If that's the way you want it."

"It is."

JENNY SHED HER CASHMERE sweater, skirt and panty hose, then pulled on heavyweight black jeans and a red-and-black flannel shirt. Thick socks and hiking boots completed her ensemble.

Grabbing a rope she had hidden in one of her suitcases, she tiptoed down the front stairs. Unbeknownst to Whit or Chaz, she had already known about the well, as well as the digging Gary had done, and she intended to check it out right now. Maybe this was the clue she needed.

She slipped quietly out the front door, taking extra care not to make any noise. Heart racing, she continued tiptoeing across the front porch, down the steps, out into the yard. Going the long way to avoid being seen out the upstairs bedrooms where Chaz was supposed to be relaxing, she headed around the big empty barns.

Once behind them, she pulled the map out of her pocket. The geological surveys said the well was a mile south of potato field number three.

Jenny climbed over the high wooden fence, then started down the field. Halfway there it occurred to her there could be snakes in this field. She broke into a jog motivated more by fear and loathing of reptiles than any desire to be in shape, and didn't stop until she reached the end of the field.

The well was there, all right, she noted with a satisfied grin. Or at least what used to be a well, she guessed.

Next to it was a huge pile of rocks, some broken, some edged with cement. The inside of the well was at least twenty feet wide, and thirty or so feet deep. The bottom was filled with shallow puddles of rainwater.

"Looks like someone just went after it with a bulldozer, doesn't it?" Chaz said, behind her.

Chapter Eight

Jenny started at the sound of Chaz's voice and almost fell into what was left of the well. Recovering her balance, she spun around angrily to face him.

"Never learn, do you?" Chaz surmised grimly, looking more furious than Jenny had ever seen him.

Her heart skipped not just one but several beats. Recovering, she thrust her chin up bravely. This was her problem, she reminded herself, not his. "How long have you been standing there?" she demanded.

"I think the question is, how long have I have been following you. And the answer is—" he approached her slowly, his chestnut brows drawn low over his stormy sea blue eyes "—ever since you left the house."

Jenny gulped around the sudden knot of tension in her throat. "Well, you can go back now."

He shook his head, his eyes as hard and uncompromising as his voice. "I don't think so."

There was something very different about him.
Something charged and electric. He looked like a
man who'd come to the end of his rope, or at least as
far down it as he intended to go. Jenny swore silently to herself. The back of her neck prickling, she
started to back up, hazarded a glance at the big hole
in the ground behind her, and circled around it
widely instead.

"Careful. I wouldn't want you falling in now,"
Chaz taunted as he matched her pace for pace.

Feeling a little like a tourist who'd unknowingly
grabbed a python by a tail, Jenny asserted with a
good deal more self-assurance than she felt, "Ha! Be
honest with me, Chaz. You'd probably like nothing
better."

"No, Jenny," Chaz corrected, "contrary to what
you think, I do not want to have to haul you out of
there. It's just a little deep," he added sarcastically.
"Or hadn't you noticed?"

"I noticed."

Chaz hazarded another glance down at the well,
then looked at her face. His gaze softened. "Hell of
a mess, isn't it?" he remarked quietly.

Jenny hoisted her rope a little higher on her
shoulder. Her heart was beating double time. "Yep,
sure is."

"Any idea why Gary was digging it up?"

Jenny shook her head, though in fact she had a
very good idea why the well had been expanded. At
least she *hoped* that was what Gary had been doing.

"You're sure?" Chaz ascertained, slowly closing the distance between them.

"Very sure." Jenny's back grazed the fence, and she started cautiously working her way sideways. She didn't like the overly protective expression on Chaz's face, or the fact he was assuming some responsibility for the problems here.

"I mean, it's a hell of a way to redig a well, isn't it? Normally, when a well runs dry, they dig deeper, not wider," Chaz continued. "Digging wider doesn't do a damn bit of good, cause you're still tapping into the same water table. You've got to go down farther, maybe twice as far. Gary may not have been a geologist, but I'm damn sure he knew that. So the question is, what was he really doing here?"

"I don't have the faintest idea."

"Really?"

"No," Jenny lied.

His blue eyes narrowed, and in that instant she saw what a powerful adversary he would be. "The answer wouldn't happen to be in those papers in your pocket, would it?" he drawled, his patience waning dangerously.

Resisting the urge to cover the papers with her hand, Jenny asked with comically exaggerated innocence, "What papers?"

His mouth thinned to a white line. "Hand them over, Jenny," Chaz directed, like a general giving orders to a foot soldier.

And have him immediately know the rest of her plans? Jenny thought, incensed. And have him try to stop her? "No way," she retorted firmly. Giving him no chance to answer, she hooked a foot on the bottom rung of the fence and hurled herself up to the top. She was halfway over it, one leg straddling either side, when he caught up with her.

"Damn you, Chaz, let me go!" Jenny ordered grimly as he clamped an arm over her hip.

"Forget it," he said through his teeth. "You are not running away from me and headlong into danger again!"

Jenny had had enough of people running her life while she was married to Gary. Then, she hadn't really known what was happening. Because Gary, like Chaz, had convinced her that he was just trying to help her out and make her life easier. Now she did know what was happening. Chaz was trying to take control. Probably, considering her past with his friend, he expected no resistance. Little did he know that from this point forward in her life, she was prepared to fight like hell against him or anyone else who tried to exert control over any part of her life. "Oh, yeah?" she said.

"Yeah," Chaz said firmly.

"We'll just see about that." Jenny swung a foot out, her heavy hiking boot connecting solidly with his middle. He swore heatedly but lost his grip on her. The split-second chink in his armor was all she needed to get the rest of the way over the fence. Then she ran full tilt for the house.

Seconds later, still swearing, he was hard on her heels. He caught up with her midfield and grabbed her around the waist. She struggled, resisting his greater strength with all her might. The next thing she knew they were rolling on the ground, tumbling over a row of bushy green potato plants. "Stop it, Jenny!"

"You stop it!" She kicked and flailed. Why couldn't he ever mind his own business?

He whipped her onto her back. Straddling her across the hips, the insides of his thighs pressing firmly, intimately, against her hips, he held her pinned to the ground. "Okay, Jenny, hand over the papers."

Pleased to see he was out of breath, too, Jenny aimed a fist at his sternum and said, "Not on your life!"

Furious at her noncompliance, he increased the pressure with his thighs and shackled both her wrists with his hands, pinning them to the ground on either side of her head. Jenny was suffused with a distinctly sexual heat everywhere they touched, and some places where they didn't.

"Last chance, Jenny. Hand them over!" he demanded.

"Take a long walk off a short pier," she advised, ignoring the growing, surprisingly sensual ache between her thighs.

"Fine," Chaz retorted tersely. "Have it your way!" He transferred both her wrists to one hand, pinned them down above her head and used his free hand to search the pocket on her shirt. Jenny squirmed wildly beneath him, but her hopes to avoid losing the papers only caused him to brush her breast with the back of his hand instead. Jenny stopped struggling immediately and stared up at him, looked at his mouth, and thought only of his kiss. And judging by the intense look in his sea blue eyes, he was remembering what it had been like to kiss her and hold her, too.

Perspiration beading on his upper lip, and an altogether different look in his eyes, he carefully withdrew the sheaf of folded papers from her breast pocket, then eyed her speculatively for a long moment. "Are you going to behave?" he asked.

Jenny was mad enough to spit nails, both for the way he'd interfered with her investigation and the macho way he was holding her down now. "What do you think?" she asked sweetly.

His eyes glimmered with an intensely male satisfaction. The type of glimmer that said he thoroughly enjoyed any battle of the sexes between them, and in fact, looked forward to the ones to come. "I think I'll just keep you here a little while longer." Oblivious to her struggles, he held her hands pinned and flattened the papers out, away from her body. While Jenny fumed and swore, he glanced through the first set, then the second, then the third and the fourth. "I'm beginning to see what all these places have in common, and you know, too, don't you, Jenny?" he said. Without warning, he bounded up and gave her a hand, pulling her gently to her feet.

"I don't have the faintest idea—"

"Cut the nonsense," he interrupted her harshly, putting out a hand to steady her as she swayed unsteadily on her feet. "Gary was digging for something," he said as his hand tightened protectively on her waist. Satisfied she was steady again, he released her. "Something he thought he'd find in the abandoned Colorado silver mine, and in this well, and in what appears to be a desert motel and a swamp."

Defeated, Jenny said nothing.

"The only question is what?" Chaz continued thoughtfully.

Jenny sighed and decided to add her two cents worth. "Well, it's not oil. I know what an oil well looks like, and this isn't the way you dig for oil."

"So the question remains," Chaz said as they started slowly for the house, "what was Gary looking for?"

"I don't know." Jenny shrugged, wishing she'd been able to solve this mystery for herself. "There's no clue on those maps. He details what type of rock is found, what type of soil, and that's it." She sighed wearily and ran a hand through her hair. "I thought at first that maybe all these places had something in common. At least I hoped they did."

"And?" Chaz stopped at the last wooden fence and gave her a boost up.

"And nothing," Jenny reported, frustrated, as she swung herself over the fence and down to the ground again. "I researched the area thoroughly, thinking there had to be something very valuable here. Otherwise, Gary wouldn't have paid so much for the land, but there has never been any history of silver being mined around here. Gold, either. And no uranium or oil."

"So what was he looking for?" Chaz asked.

Jenny shrugged, not sure whether she was more irritated or perplexed by Gary's actions. "Who knows?"

She and Chaz were silent as they crossed the last hundred yards to the house. "So why didn't you tell me all this to begin with?" Chaz asked.

"Because," Jenny said heatedly, wishing he would stop trying to take such an active role in running her life, "this isn't your problem, Chaz, it's mine."

Chaz paused on the porch. He gave her a telling look. "Yours, and who else's, Jenny?"

Jenny's heart began a slow, heavy beat. Clearly Chaz was very worried about something. "What do you mean?"

He held open the door. Jenny stepped past him, the narrow space forcing her to get close enough to smell the spicy scent of his after-shave.

"Did Gary tell anyone else about these properties?" Chaz followed her on inside.

Jenny glanced at him. She wished he wouldn't look at her so intensely, as if they were the only two people on earth. "I don't know," she replied uncomfortably. Searching for something to do with her hands, she stuck them into the pockets of her black jeans. "I don't think so. Why do you ask?"

"Because." Chaz stepped nearer and his voice dropped a confidential notch. "It's obvious someone knows about them."

Very conscious of the way Chaz towered over her by a good six or seven inches, Jenny tilted her head back and regarded him warily. "The utilities."

"Yes. Someone turned on the phone and the electricity, and they did it in your name."

Jenny told herself the only reason she felt so disconcerted was because she and Chaz thought so much alike. It had nothing to do with the attraction she felt simmering just beneath the surface. "Well, maybe it was my accountant."

Deciding the more physical space she could put between herself and Chaz, the better, Jenny strode into the kitchen and went straight to the phone. She picked up the receiver resolutely. "At least I can check."

"My accountant didn't do it," Jenny said several minutes later.

So who did? Chaz wondered.

Because Jenny looked as if she was about to faint, Chaz pulled out a ladder-back chair and guided her gently but firmly toward the seat. "Maybe you'd better sit down, Jen." He paused as she got situated, then asked gently, "What else did your accountant say?"

Jenny rubbed the back of her neck. She raked the white edges of her teeth across the softness of her lower lip. "You're not going to believe this. I had an offer on the Colorado property today. Fifteen percent over what I paid."

Chaz's gut tightened. Every protective instinct he had rushed to the fore. "From whom?" he demanded.

Jenny shrugged her shoulders and looked even more baffled and distressed by the mysterious turn of events. "That's just it. The realtor up there who sold the property to Gary wouldn't say. He told my accountant that the prospective buyer prefers to remain anonymous at this time."

Chaz pulled out a chair, turned it around so the back faced Jenny and sank into it backward. He folded his arms over the top rung. Jenny might be too stubborn and independent to admit it, but she needed help here. "What are you going to do?"

"I don't know." Jenny rubbed at an imaginary spot on her jeans, stroking the black fabric from midthigh to knee. She stared at her leg. "I could get part of my money back, if I sold it."

"But?" Chaz asked, hearing the hesitation in her low, gentle voice.

Jenny lifted her head and looked directly into his eyes. She inhaled deeply before she spoke, the reflexive action visibly lifting the softness of her breasts. "Don't you think it's a little funny that someone would want to pay over market value for that impossible-to-get-to place if it weren't worth anything?"

Ignoring the way his lower half tightened whenever he looked at Jenny too long, Chaz tore his gaze from the tumble of golden blond hair that fell over Jenny's shoulders and made her look as if she had just gotten out of bed. His mood both grim and worried, he pushed to his feet, walked to the refrigerator and yanked it open. Reaching inside, he pulled out a half-full gallon of skim milk. God knows he didn't want to upset Jenny any further, but he figured it was time she knew.

"Yeah, I think it's strange," Chaz said. "Almost as peculiar as this." He handed the carton of milk to Jenny. "Check out the date."

Jenny stared at the date stamped on the label. "This milk loses its freshness nine days from now," she said, in awe.

"Which can only mean," Chaz surmised bluntly, "that it was purchased in the last day or so."

"And then brought here and put in the refrigerator," Jenny deduced. New color flooded her cheeks. Her dark eyes fairly danced with the excitement of discovery. "But by whom, Chaz?"

Chaz leaned back against the counter for a moment, his arms folded at his waist, and regarded her casually. "I was hoping you could tell me."

Unfortunately, Jenny looked as puzzled as he felt. Chaz went back to the refrigerator and opened it again.

"Anything else in there?" Jenny asked, from behind him.

Able to feel the heat of her voluptuous body next to his, Chaz replied, albeit a little huskily, "Only a carton of yogurt and two apples."

Jenny leaned over his shoulder. She exhaled her frustration at the limited clues they had. The warm, sexy whisper of her breath brushed his neck. "Are they fresh?" she asked.

Chaz examined them both, then turned to face her. He handed the apple and yogurt to Jenny. "You tell me."

She eyed them carefully, looking all the more disturbed, then handed them back. "So someone was just here," she said softly, and lifted her dark eyes to him.

"As well as at the lodge in Colorado," Chaz said, noting for the first time how blond and thick and long her lashes were, even without mascara.

Jenny blinked and bit her lip again. "What do you mean?"

Chaz reached past Jenny and calmly put the fruit, yogurt and milk back into the refrigerator. "When we got there, the ashes in the grate were warm," he reported as he shut the appliance door with a soft thud. His lips compressed grimly at the memory. "The end of one of the logs was wet."

Jenny's gaze narrowed. Her dark eyes took on an incensed, fiery light. "Wait a minute, Chaz. Are you telling me you noticed that and didn't tell me?"

Chaz had done what he thought was best at the time. Recalling how exhausted Jenny had been from their eight-hour trek up the mountainside, how she'd flirted with hysteria upon simply seeing the lodge Gary had purchased, he stood by his decision. "I didn't want to worry you," he explained.

Jenny's mouth tightened until he could no longer see the bow-shaped curves of each lip. "Damn it, Chaz," she demanded emotionally, "how could you!"

"How could I what?" Chaz followed her through the parlor and halfway up the stairs.

Jenny whirled to face him. She looked as if she were sorely tempted to attack. "How could you have kept that from me?" She stopped, with the wall at her back.

Chaz stared at her incredulously, unable to understand what she was so upset about. "I didn't tell you because I didn't want to worry you unduly at that point."

"Well, for your information, I don't need your protection!" Jenny said, slamming her tightly clenched fists against her thighs. "A man's protection is what got me in this mess in the first place!"

She pivoted away from him and continued up the stairs, taking them two at a time.

Chaz chased after her. He could only imagine how Gary had rationalized his behavior to Jenny, but Gary's underhanded treachery didn't have anything to do with him. When she calmed down, Jenny would realize that, too. *If* she calmed down, he amended. "Jenny—"

"Just leave me alone, Chaz!" Jenny's boots echoed on the polished wood floor as she headed resolutely for the off-limits territory of her bedroom. "Don't talk to me! Don't say another word!"

Suddenly Chaz had had enough. Not just of Jenny, but of the hundreds of people who had shut him out and snubbed him over the years. He was tired of being looked at as if he were somehow less of a person than someone like Jenny because of where he'd started. That misperception was intensified because he didn't want a home in the suburbs, a wife, 1.7 kids and a high-powered career. And it hurt even more to have Jenny look at him that way.

He caught up with Jenny in two strides, stopping her before she could slam the bedroom door. "Hold it right there, Jenny. You may not like this mess Gary left you in any more than I do, but like it or not we're in this together—if for no other reason than you came to me for help!"

Jenny flattened a hand on his chest and tried to shove him out of her doorway. "I also told you that you could go!"

Chaz held firm. "I'm not a servant who can be dismissed, Jen! And while we're on the subject," he continued, closing his fingers about her wrist, "don't walk away from me when we're in the middle of an important discussion."

Jenny shook off his grip and removed her hand from his chest. "Then you stop trying to censor what you think I should or should not know!" she retorted, looking equally upset.

Chaz lounged against the open door. Glaring down at her, he made an effort to quell his rising temper, which was fast approaching the dangerous level. "You're telling me you would've slept easier had you known someone was ahead of us in this little game of cat and mouse!" he asked. "You're telling me you would've slept better had you known that right this very minute you could very well be in physical danger?"

Jenny's mouth dropped open in a round O of surprise.

The color left her face.

The next thing he knew their mouths were fused together and the tension that had been building the entire trip exploded in one kiss. The world around them narrowed in a red-hot blaze of passion, until Chaz was aware only of the heat and the softness of her lips, and the sweet peppermint flavor of her mouth. But it wasn't just his body that had been affected. His heart had gone on a rampage, too. It was pounding wildly, telling him this was something different. That Jenny was different from everyone who had come before.

And Jenny, he thought tenderly as their kiss deepened and grew yet more exciting and complex... Jenny had been affected, too. He could tell by the ragged meter of her breathing, the pounding of her heart. He could tell by the unsteady way she clung to him, her legs and breasts and tummy all fluid and hot against him. She wanted him, too, as desperately as he wanted her.

His temper fading, his desire soaring, he brought her closer still. She moaned softly in her throat and curled her fingers in the hair at the nape of his neck. She surged against him, the softness of her breasts crushed against the flat hard plane of his chest. Imagining what it would be like to hold all of her against all of him, without the frustrating barrier of clothing between them, he groaned against her mouth, tilted his hips and pressed into her, lifting her slightly against the door at her back. She moaned with the feel of his arousal at the vee of her thighs, and became even more wild and wanton. His own pulse pounding, he kissed her again until she was limp and acquiescent against him.

Just when she was his for the taking, it happened. His conscience demanded to be heard. He dragged his mouth from hers, sighed, and for the first and only time in his life wished to hell he wasn't quite so gallant at heart. Again he closed his eyes, knowing if he looked deep into her sable brown eyes and saw desire he wasn't going to be able to do the right thing. "Jenny," he began as she buried her face in his neck.

"Oh, Chaz," she whispered back, her breath soughing damply out against his collarbone. She clutched at his shoulders like a woman who was in full command of her senses. "It's been so long since anyone's—" Her voice broke unexpectedly, and she lifted her face to his.

"Much too long," he agreed as he bent to kiss her hungrily once again, his hands moving all the while, dispensing first with the buttons on her black-and-red flannel shirt, then the front clasp of her bra. He pushed the cloth aside and stopped, stunned by the beauty of her pale golden skin. Her breasts were perfect and full and round, their centers tight and pink. Unable to help himself, he brushed his knuckles across her nipples and watched as they tightened all the more. When he lowered his head to kiss first one rigid peak and then the other, she gasped.

"Chaz—" She stirred against him restlessly, her dark eyes glazed with passion, both her hands coming up to rest against his chest. She looked at him, her expression stunned and confused. "I, we...we can't—"

"Can't?" Chaz stared at her in astonishment. He wanted her so badly he ached. "Jenny—"

"No, Chaz." Jenny flattened her hands across his chest and pushed away from him. "No."

Chaz let her go, because it was what she wanted, and stepped back. Jenny turned away from him, the horror at what she'd just done dawning on her face. "Oh, God. I can't believe I—" She pulled the edges of her blouse together. "We never should have done that. Not in a million years—"

"Like hell we shouldn't have," Chaz said gruffly, knowing, even if Jenny didn't, that this was no time to have regrets. What had just happened, happened. There was no use wishing it hadn't, particularly since this had been inevitable, from the very first time they kissed. When Jenny calmed down, she would realize that, too. One day, and he hoped it was soon, they would make love the way they were meant to make love.

Sensing Jenny wasn't ready to hear that, however, he decided to focus on the things they could more easily address. Like the trouble Gary had left her. "Look, Jen, nothing of earth-shattering significance has happened here. It's nothing to beat yourself up about."

Jenny sent him a withering glare.

Chaz had never been so tongue-tied, or behaved so ineptly, in his life. Then again, the stakes had never been so high, either. Jenny was taking this all wrong, and it would be hard as hell to convince her that his intentions here had been strictly honorable. Swearing silently to himself, Chaz tried again. "What I mean is, what just happened is nothing that can't be undone."

Her glare turned lethal. Jenny regarded him shrewdly. "I can certainly see why you'd feel that way," she remarked with a tight smile. Her dark eyes ignited in fiery accusation. "Since all you've ever cared about is getting me in the sack, anyway. Now that you see it's not going to happen, however, maybe you'll leave me alone!" Whirling, she stomped into her bedroom.

Chaz strode after her defiantly and watched, mesmerized, as she jerked a brush through her hair, swiftly restoring order to the silky golden curls. Wanting her to know the full extent of his commitment to her, he announced gently, "For the record, Jen, I'm not going anywhere until you're safely back in Dallas."

"A little late to be so tender and gallant, isn't it, Chaz?" Jenny snapped as she tossed down her brush. Not waiting for his reply, she marched past him and headed back down the stairs.

He caught up with her in the kitchen, clamped a hand on her shoulder and spun her around. "Be honest, Jen," he said, scanning her from head to toe, memorizing every delectable inch. Whether she wanted him to know it or not, Jenny was a very passionate woman. She had also very nearly been his. He frowned and continued bluntly, "You wanted that necking session to happen as much as I did."

Her chin lifted a haughty notch. "If you believe that, you're really dreaming."

He stared at her in exasperation, feeling as if he were dealing with a stranger, not the sweet, loving woman who had just kissed him with all her heart.

Was she acting this way because she expected him to hurt and betray her the way Gary had? "Jenny—" Chaz began, perplexed.

Jenny's expression became even more forbidding. "Do us both a favor, Chaz."

Chaz stared at her, knowing more than anything he just wanted her to be happy. "Anything," he promised softly.

"That necking session just now? Forget it ever happened."

"WHAT DO YOU MEAN, my offer was refused?" Lillian McCarry said over the crackling of the long-distance lines. She put down the coring she'd been studying, wrapped it up and slid the metal and rock back into the protective case.

"Just what I said," the Colorado realtor replied. "Jenny Olson's accountant said she wanted nothing to do with it. She's not selling."

This wasn't fair! Jenny Olson hadn't done all the work! Lillian and Gary had! "Did she say why she won't?" Lillian asked tensely.

"No. Listen, do you want me to try again? Or look for something else in the area?"

"No. I want that hunting lodge and all the land around it. I thought I had made that clear."

"If it's just a hunting lodge you want, or even an old abandoned silver mine," the realtor replied, "you could do better."

Lillian didn't see how. "Make another offer," she said tersely.

"You're kidding, right?"

Lillian ignored his surprise. "This time offer eighteen percent over the original sale price, and if she won't jump at that, try twenty."

There was a long silence on the other end of the line. "You're sure about this?" the realtor asked finally.

Damn sure, Lillian thought. One way or another, no matter what roadblocks Jenny Olson put up or how difficult she proved to be, Lillian was getting her property back. "Don't question me," Lillian advised. "Just do it."

Chapter Nine

"So now what?" Chaz asked the next morning as they packed up and prepared to leave the Idaho farmhouse.

Jenny carried her suitcase and vanity case down the stairs. "I don't know about you," she retorted with an indifferent toss of her golden hair. "*I'm* going on to Las Vegas."

"To gamble or look at property?"

"Guess."

For not the first time, Chaz wondered just how much of Jenny's trust fund Gary had spent. Normally he would say something like that would be none of his business, but in this situation, he wondered if maybe he shouldn't make it his, and find out as soon as possible exactly how much financial trouble Jenny was really in. His gut instinct told him quite a lot.

His speculation was further fueled by the fact that Jenny was normally a very calm, levelheaded woman, her penchant for beautiful clothes in any and all conditions aside. Yet on this trip she had behaved almost irrationally at times. She had railed at Gary and actually cried in front of Chaz, plus suffered the embarrassment of having her credit card declined in the Denver airport. Even he, with his financial circumstances as shaky as they sometimes were, hadn't had that happen to him.

Chaz fell into step beside Jenny and asked, as if it were no big deal, "Gary bought land in Nevada, too?"

Jenny's mouth tightened. She knew Chaz was just trying to be helpful with his demonstrated interest in her private affairs, but she really wished he would mind his own business. "You got it." She watched as Chaz made several trips up and down the stairs, carrying her half-dozen suitcases to the porch.

"Did he buy property anywhere else?" Chaz asked.

Jenny carefully examined the bottles of lotions and soaps in her vanity case before carefully shutting the lid. "Yes. He did."

Chaz paused and looked at her, his sea blue eyes glimmering with amusement. "Are you going to tell me or am I going to have to drag it out of you?"

She gave him a look that was not at all appreciative of his persistent questioning. Chaz grinned at the show of temper in her eyes.

"Louisiana."

Chaz paused, wondering what kind of getup Jenny had brought with her to wear there. Since she'd worn western clothes out West, he figured she'd probably wear something hopelessly frilly and feminine in the Deep South. Something that would make his blood run even hotter than it already was. He shifted his weight, trying to ease the pressure in the front of his jeans. "I suppose you're going to look at that, too," he surmised.

"Yep."

Still grinning at the single-word answers she was giving him, probably in a hopelessly ineffectual effort to discourage him, Chaz set his own duffel bag and backpack next to the door. He stuck his hands into the pockets of his jeans and regarded her affably. "Then that's where I'm going, too."

Jenny strode into the kitchen, where she checked the stove and coffeepot to make sure they were turned off. "Chaz, you don't have to keep following me," she said, exasperated.

"Yeah, I know." He followed her back out into the living room, marveling at the changes in her in just the past few days. She'd always been slightly aloof where he was concerned, out of bounds. But she'd never been quite this single-minded. He liked the new Jenny, even though her growing recklessness worried him. She was so used to always getting what she wanted, she couldn't accept that Gary's wheeling and dealing might not have a happy ending. "I want to, though," he said.

Jenny picked up her purse and rifled through it for her keys. She was wearing a hot-pink shirtdress that ended just above her knees. The wide belt emphasized her waist, which was looking a little slimmer every day, and the straight skirt set off the gentle curve of her hips. She had on white stockings but had forsaken her usual dressy flats or heels in favor of her high-topped Reeboks and sweatsocks. He found the combination irresistibly sexy. "Why do you want to tag along?" Jenny asked with a beleaguered sigh. *So you can kiss me again? We can't let that happen.*

Chaz allowed his eyes to drift over the softness of her golden hair. It smelled as fresh and fragrant as the rest of her. If only she were as open to romance as she looked. "Because you're lacking the common sense gene," he teased.

"Ha!" Jenny started out the door. Chaz followed her, waiting as she paused to lock up behind them.

He transferred his bags to one hand and lounged against the frame. "If I hadn't come along when I did last night, who knows if you ever would've gotten out of that well."

Jenny rolled her eyes, slipped her key into her purse and started for their cars at a decisive clip. "I wasn't going into the well."

"Right." Chaz fell into step beside her as they began the process of ferrying Jenny's half-dozen suitcases from the porch to her rental car. "You were just carrying along that clothesline for lasso practice, in case one of the potato plants got away."

Jenny regarded him for a long moment, her dark eyes glowing vivaciously all the while. "It wasn't a clothesline," she corrected drolly, "it was a rope."

Chaz stopped at the rear of her rental car and unlocked her trunk. "Beg to differ with you, Jen, that was a clothesline."

Jenny opened her own car door and tossed her purse inside. She faced him over the hood. "So what if it was?"

"So it wasn't strong enough to support your weight," he explained.

Jenny leaned a hip against the side of the car and watched him wrestle with her suitcases, in an attempt to fit them all in. "I didn't use it anyway," she reminded.

He paused and glanced up at her. "You would've."

"No." Jenny dropped her arms in exasperation. "I wouldn't have." She paused as he finally fit everything in and shut the trunk, then stepped back and picked up his own bags. "Not when I saw how filthy and muddy that well was," Jenny continued. "In fact, if you hadn't come along I— Chaz, you dropped something."

"What?" He turned to see her kneeling next to a postcard. Jenny picked it up. On the front was a beachscape from the Bahamas. On the back was a handwritten note.

"It's a postcard," she said. "From someone named . . . Regina Thorpe."

"Oh yeah?" Chaz asked as he unlocked the trunk of his rental car and stowed his gear in the trunk. "What does it say?"

Jenny read, with an increasing lack of expression in her low voice, *"Thanks for being there. I couldn't have pulled it all together without you."*

Chaz smiled. Jenny didn't.

"Old girlfriend?" she asked, hating the possessiveness coursing through her, a possessiveness she had no right to feel where Chaz was concerned. Kisses or no kisses!

"Not exactly," Chaz said.

Jenny paused, her hand on the handle of her car door. I have no claim on this man, she reminded herself defiantly.

"I dated her for a while. In the end, we were just friends."

Jenny wanted to believe that was all there was to the card. Her experience with Gary had taught her to look beyond the surface of everything, and everyone. "So why is she sending you postcards from the Bahamas?" she asked lightly, still holding the sea blue eyes.

Chaz shrugged again, and continued to hold her gaze. "Because she's now a scuba instructor there and likes to keep in touch."

Jenny nodded. "I see." The truth was Chaz probably had a woman in every port, Jenny thought grumpily. He probably picked them up on his adventures. He was probably trying to pick her up now—on this little jaunt—to add to his collection.

"Regina went through a really rough time, Jen."

We all go through rough times, Chaz. That doesn't mean you had to be her Sir Galahad. Out loud, Jenny queried him brightly, like one of those chirpy morning talk show hostesses interviewing a guest. "How so?"

Chaz frowned, as if just the memory pained him, too. "Her first husband emptied their bank account and walked out on her."

Because it was too painful for her to continue to hold his gaze without revealing more of her growing feelings for him than she cared to, Jenny dropped her gaze from Chaz's face, to the rumpled cotton shirt and jeans he wore. Funny, she thought, how he always looked so good in simple, clean but unironed, cotton shirts and ruggedly constructed khaki slacks or jeans. She swallowed hard. She shouldn't be attracted to Chaz. She lifted her head. "Kind of like what Gary did to me, you mean?"

Chaz frowned. "I didn't say that."

"No." Jenny sighed. "But you were thinking it."

Chaz mulled that over. "I guess you're right. Anyway, the message on the card refers to the fact that I stood by her and gave her a shoulder to cry on when she needed it."

And how often had Regina needed that shoulder to cry on, Jenny wondered jealously. The image of Chaz with another woman was not a pleasant one.

"Eventually, as I knew she would," Chaz continued informatively, with no more feeling than if he
were reciting the letters of the alphabet, "she pulled
her life together again. And we went our separate
ways."

Jenny handed Chaz back the postcard and
watched as he slid it into his backpack pocket once
again. "But you're still in touch." Did that mean
Regina still cared for him, that only Chaz had lost
interest in the relationship? Would the same thing
happen to her if she were to become involved with
Chaz? Would he flee the moment she no longer
needed a shoulder to cry on?

Chaz shrugged. "Sure, we see each other now and
then. As friends," he emphasized flatly. He looked
at Jenny steadily, wanting to let her know that, unlike Gary, she could trust him to tell her the truth
about his life. "You'd probably like her, if you met
her."

Jenny swallowed, leaned back against the trunk of
her car and crossed one ankle over the other. "You
really enjoy helping women in distress, don't you?"
she asked, her gaze spearing him with laser accuracy.

He shrugged, not sure what she was getting at. He
only knew it wasn't a compliment. He wasn't
ashamed of anything he'd done for other women,
including Regina, no matter how unsettled or jealous it made Jenny feel.

"Sure, I feel a great deal of satisfaction whenever I help someone," Chaz admitted candidly, closing the distance between them. "Just like you probably feel a great deal of satisfaction when you help someone in the course of your volunteer work at the children's hospital."

"Somehow, Chaz, I don't think it's quite the same thing," Jenny said, giving him a long steady look. She jerked open the car door with unnecessary force and ducked inside.

I AM NOT JUST another one of his damsels in distress, Jenny told herself over and over on the long drive back to the Boise airport.

Of course not, you're something worse: a burden, the widow of his late best friend.

Thanks heaps, she told herself wryly.

Look, just enjoy being with him while you can, her hedonistic side argued. After all, how often do you have a sexy hunk like Chaz chasing you all over the country, offering you his protection? How often do you get to play the damsel in distress to his Sir Galahad?

Not often, Jenny knew. But she also knew she didn't want to be used again, or courted for anything other than herself. And she was very much afraid that Chaz was courting her for reasons that simply wouldn't hold up, long term. That once her plight was over he'd lose interest in her and be on his merry way. Only she had the feeling she wouldn't lose interest in him nearly so fast, if at all.

Jenny sighed. If only she still had her money, she wouldn't be in this predicament! Unfortunately, she didn't have her money, and unless she managed to work a miracle, the sad truth was, she might never get even a fraction of it back.

"THIS ISN'T SUCH a big deal, Jenny," Chaz counseled a frazzled Jenny long hours later.

"Says you," she snapped at him as they exited the Boise airport terminal. "I, however, do not enjoy the prospect of spending yet another night in Idaho." Especially when she had so much to do in Louisiana and Nevada.

Chaz tried to look on the bright side as he stowed their luggage in yet another trunk. "At least we're booked on a flight out first thing tomorrow," he said as he jammed the overflow into the back seat. At least they were sharing a rental car this time, instead of driving in separate vehicles.

"Big whoop." Jenny tapped her foot on the pavement, looking as if she were about to explode. "I want to fly to Las Vegas tonight."

"So do I," Chaz sympathized, moving past her to unlock the passenger door with the key. "Unfortunately, there are no other available flights to Las Vegas tonight, so we have no choice but to check into a hotel, and take the first flight out tomorrow morning. C'mon, buck up," he coaxed, wishing he could see her sunny smile again. He squeezed her hand warmly, as well as the key resting between their palms. "It won't be so bad. We'll be there soon enough anyway."

Fortunately, there was a huge Holiday Inn near the airport. "Will this be a single or a double?" the clerk asked.

"Two singles," Chaz said. "And make mine the cheapest you've got."

"Mine, too," Jenny was quick to add, and handed over her credit card.

Chaz shot her an astonished look. In all the time Jenny had been married to Gary, he'd never known her to travel less than first class. Yet in the past couple of days, he'd seen her fly coach when first class was still available. He'd seen her eat a hamburger in a restaurant, when she normally would've ordered a steak. At first he'd chalked it up to lack of interest and appetite. But now suddenly he had to wonder at the real reason behind her sudden change in tastes. Surely, he thought, she would have at least requested a suite, since the hotel they were staying in was bound to be modest by her old-money standards.

"You sure you're going to be comfortable in a single?" Chaz asked, handing over his card, too.

Before Jenny had the chance to answer, the clerk said, "Ms. Olson, I'm sorry to interrupt, but there's a problem with your card. It's been declined."

Jenny's cheeks turned bright pink with embarrassment. "Oh dear." She fished in her purse for another, and brought out yet another card. "Try this."

Chaz's heart went out to Jenny as the two of them waited in an awkward silence, for the second card to be processed. The clerk came back. "I'm sorry, Ms. Olson, but your MasterCard's been declined, too."

Chaz had tried not to embarrass Jenny. He knew how much she wanted to handle every detail of her affairs these days. But he'd witnessed enough. "Listen, Jen, I'll get your room," he said to her, then turned to the clerk authoritatively, "Put it on my card, please."

"No." Jenny's adamant tone surprised both Chaz and the clerk. "I'll pay for the room," she insisted firmly, her cheeks an even brighter pink. "In cash." As Chaz and the clerk watched, she carefully counted out the money and handed it over. Looking, Chaz noticed, as if she were really loath to part with every single cent.

Chaz waited until Jenny had unlocked the door to her room before he spoke. "Okay, Jen. It's true confession time here. What's going on with you?"

Jenny picked up two of her suitcases and headed inside. Chaz brought in the other four. "I don't know what you mean."

"What I mean is that's not exactly the first credit card you've had declined on this trip."

Jenny gave him a sharp look, as if she wondered how he could have been so uncouth to mention it. Her gaze averted from his probing one, she picked up the empty ice bucket and took a handful of quarters from her purse. "Keeping track, are you?"

He barred her way to the door before she could exit the cramped hotel room. "How much trouble are you in?"

Ignoring his question, Jenny ducked under his arm, headed out the door and down the hall to the vending machines. Still pointedly ignoring his presence, she began helping herself to some ice.

The seconds dragged on, each as tense as the one preceding it.

To Jenny's obvious dismay, Chaz refused to give in, or give up.

Aware that he wasn't likely to go away until he had an answer, Jenny pretended to study the choices of cola. She supposed miserably that she should be used to being humiliated by her lack of funds by now, but she wasn't, not in the least. It was only fitting that the man whose opinion she cared most about was witnessing every degrading second of her decline into financial ruin. What was that saying, she wondered wearily. That pride goeth before a fall? Well, maybe it was time she let go of the last of her pride, at least where Chaz was concerned, even if it was going to be one of the most difficult things she had ever done in her life.

"All right! If you absolutely must know—"

"Trust me, Jen. I must know." Chaz hovered over her like a mother hen.

"I'm down to my last thousand."

Chaz swore. Jenny set the filled ice bucket on top of the ice machine and fed quarters to the soft drink machine. When they clinked in, she punched the button that said Classic Coke. The can rolled down to the pickup slot with a rumble and a thud. Jenny picked up the can and offered Chaz a couple of quarters.

He looked at her tenderly. "Maybe I should be loaning you the change for this machine."

"Forget it, Chaz. I may be teetering on the edge of total financial ruin, but I can still afford to buy you a Coke. Besides," Jenny said as she fed more change to the machine and got Chaz the Dr Pepper she knew he preferred, "I'll be all right once I resell the properties Gary bought and pay my bills. Maybe I won't be as rich as I was. Maybe I'll even have to take a salaried job for a while. But, I'll manage."

Chaz waited until they were in her room again before he said gently, "It terrifies you, doesn't it, being without money?"

Jenny kicked off her shoes and took the shrink-wrap off the plastic glass. She looked at Chaz sagely. "How would you feel in my place?"

Chaz watched as she added ice to her drink and sank into one of the upholstered chairs on either side of the small round table. "Why didn't you tell me?"

Jenny slouched down until she could rest her neck on the back of the chair. She closed her eyes. "The same reason I didn't tell anyone else. Because I didn't want you to know. It's just too darn embarrassing." Sitting up again, she took a sip of her Coke.

Chaz took a long draft of his Dr Pepper, preferring to drink straight from the can. "I would've helped."

Jenny smiled at him gently. "You helped anyway."

"I would've helped more," Chaz insisted.

Jenny got up to pace the room restlessly. "What else could you have done?"

Chaz tried not to notice how provocatively her hips moved beneath her skirt. "I don't know. Introduced you to a rich beau?" He grinned.

Jenny smiled at the absurdity of that.

Knowing he was onto something that would lighten her mood, if not necessarily his, Chaz reminded her teasingly, "You never said what kind of guy you wanted to date, you know."

Jenny's glass halted halfway to her lips, giving Chaz hope that maybe she'd had second thoughts about asking him to help her find someone else to date. "You never asked."

His eyes held hers. *Tell me you've changed your mind,* he thought. "I'm asking now."

You, Chaz, Jenny thought. *As crazy as it sounds, I want to date you.* Because, however, that wasn't an option, Jenny resumed her nervous pacing and said evasively, "To tell you the truth, Chaz, I don't know what kind of man I want to date. I haven't really thought about it."

Guess that rules me out, Chaz thought grimly. "So think now." His voice had an edge.

Telling himself this conversation would be easier to endure if he were busier, Chaz opened a drawer and took out some hotel stationery and a complimentary pen. Think about the other guys she is going to date, he urged himself sternly, and not about the way that shirt outlines the voluptuousness of her breasts.

"Do you want them to be from a similar background?"

Jenny looked at him, for a second staring like a deer frozen in the headlights of an oncoming car. She recovered more swiftly than he, moistening her lips and replying, "That would probably be nice, yes."

Chaz swore inwardly, wishing he had never started this ridiculous game. It might help take Jenny's mind off being broke, but it was doing insane things to his. He couldn't remember ever feeling so jealous, with so little reason. "Do you want them to be rich?"

Jenny busied herself adding more soda and more ice to her plastic cup. Her back to him, she replied casually, "I hadn't thought about that, either, but I suppose that's a good idea." Chaz glanced up. Their eyes clashed.

Jenny continued frankly, "I would like the next man I get involved with to have his own money, if for no other reason than I won't have to worry about him stealing mine. Assuming—" she shrugged carelessly, as if it were no longer much of a concern to her, "—that I get it back."

"Oh, you'll get it back." Jenny quirked a brow. "I have faith in you," Chaz continued. *And faith in me.* He wrote "rich" on his list, and resisted, with effort, following "rich" with "bastard." Resting his pen against his thigh, he said, "So what else?"

"I don't know." Jenny shrugged, looking as if this was of no more consequence to her than what color bedspreads were on their beds. "They should be polite. Well mannered. Well groomed."

Chaz looked back at his list, his expression businesslike. "Anything else?"

"Well," Jenny hedged, getting into it a little more without warning. "I'd prefer they not have a bad track record with women. I'm not interested in someone who's been married and divorced five times."

Chaz grinned as he made note of that, too. "What about just two or three divorces? Is that okay?"

Jenny laughed. Color flowed into her cheeks, making her look even prettier. "Stop teasing me," she chided.

Chaz rubbed his jaw. "Can't help it. Your list is so...well, interesting, to say the least." He stood and waved the list at her. He was glad for the chance to stretch and get a little closer to her. "I hate to say it, Jen, but anyone who fits this profile sounds about as exciting as the summer reruns on TV." He closed the distance between them slowly and looked down at her upturned face and searched for any clue of her real feelings, even those he knew she would prefer to keep hidden. "Are you sure you wouldn't just rather have a strictly physical relationship with some-one—" *like me* "—and forget about trying to find Husband Number Two?"

"No," Jenny said softly, stubbornly. Tired of pacing, she sat down on the edge of the bed. "If and when I ever get to the point where I'm willing to get deeply involved with someone again, then yes, I think I would want to be married again, Chaz."

He came over and sat down beside her. The mattress shifted with his weight. To Jenny's surprise, she felt a little like a ship captain who'd just found port in a storm. "How come?"

He already knew the worst about her. He might as well know the rest, Jenny reasoned. "Because I want commitment," she admitted bravely, without apology, daring to look directly into his sea blue eyes. She finished with a conviction that came straight from her heart. "And a real commitment, the kind you can bank on through thick and thin, means marriage, Chaz."

Chaz broke into an easy grin. "Then I say go for it, Jen."

It would have been better for her ego that he be madly jealous, instead of such an enthusiastic matchmaker. Jenny was sorry she had ever started this, though in Colorado it had seemed like a good idea.

They both drifted a little, alone in their thoughts. Finally Jenny looked at Chaz and realized how much she was coming to rely on him. Not just for his companionship or his skills in adventuring or even his very male protection of her. But just to be there for her and with her, talking to her, aggravating her, questioning, tagging along. She'd never met a man like Chaz. Unconventional in some ways, such as his choice of career and life-style, and a throwback in others, such as the way he treated, and protected, her. He didn't look at what clothes she wore, or what she drove, or where she lived. He didn't make any judgments about her, save to tell her when she wasn't being honest with herself or with him.

Jenny couldn't say the same about a lot of the so-called friends she had left back in Dallas.

"Chaz?"

"Hmm?" He looked up, appearing to be as content just to be with her as she was to be with him. His expression made Jenny wish for one reckless second that they hadn't done the proper thing and gotten separate rooms, but saved costs, said to hell with propriety, and bunked in together.

"You really don't care, do you?" Jenny said, a little awed.

Chaz grinned at her affectionately. "About what?"

"That I'm about down to my last dime."

Chaz put his hand over hers and squeezed. "Your money isn't what makes you irresistible, Jenny."

Jenny wished she could believe that. Just as she wished she and Chaz would someday have a real chance to be together. "Oh, yeah? Then what does?" she challenged quietly.

For a moment, he looked at a loss. Finally Chaz shook his head, released his grip on her hand, got up and walked away. "I don't know if I can put it into words. There's just something about you...and while we're on the subject of you, Jen, there's something I need to say." Chaz paused. "When I asked to borrow money from you, I had no idea what your personal circumstances were." His eyes searched hers, demanding both understanding and forgiveness. "I never would've put you on the spot like that if I'd had any idea."

"I know—" Jenny said softly. Maybe she hadn't then, but she did now. "I'm sorry Gary let you down, Chaz," Jenny said, meaning it more than she had ever meant anything in her life. "I'm sorry he put us both in the position where I had to let you down, too."

Chaz shook his head, cutting her off. "It's not your fault, Jen."

But it was, Jenny thought, because she should've been more aware. She should have paid attention to her finances. She should have listened to everyone and made sure her money was safe, not just once, but on a regular basis. But she hadn't. And now, whatever happened, she still had to go on, rich or poor. Nevertheless, Jenny hadn't given up hope that she could still turn things around. Maybe she hadn't found anything in Colorado or Idaho to help her, but they still had two more properties to explore.

"If I ever do get my money back, or at least enough of it where I can make a loan, the eighty thousand is yours," she promised, knowing it was a loan she'd be glad to make.

Chaz's eyes softened. "You don't have to do that, Jen," he said.

"I know, but I want to, Chaz." More than you'll ever know.

Chapter Ten

Jenny cut the car motor and sat staring in stunned silence at the zebra-striped motel rising out of the Nevada desert. "This can't be the place." No one painted motels black and white with hot-pink trim!

"Maybe it's not as bad as it looks," Chaz said helpfully as he got out of the car.

Jenny turned and shot him a look before emerging to stand beside him. There was no doubt this was the address. She had checked it twice. "How can it not be as bad as it looks?" She elbowed him, directing his attention to the unlit neon sign overhead. "'Jungle Fever Motel, Rooms By The Hour.' Now I ask you. Does this sound like a place where you'd want to bring your kids?"

"You're right," Chaz agreed with mock graveness. "I don't see a playground. A pool, either, actually."

Jenny rolled her eyes in exasperation. "Of course they don't have a pool. I doubt anyone ever leaves their rooms long enough to take a swim. And if they did ... well, never mind what the kind of customer who'd come here would be liable to do in the swimming pool." She groaned, thinking of the horrors of managing a sleazy place like this, not to mention actually owning it. What would her friends in Dallas think if word of this ever got out?

Chaz grinned. "Got an active mind, don't you, Jen?"

As well as an active libido, Jenny thought, recalling how ardently she'd responded to his kisses the night before last. "I guess we might as well go in," she said finally.

Chaz shrugged. "Might as well."

The desk clerk was an older guy who wore suspenders on his pants and a cardigan sweater over his shirt and looked a lot like Robert Young in his "Father Knows Best" days. Jenny introduced herself and Chaz. Briefly, without getting into any of the details of her marriage, she explained to Mr. Selwyn that Gary had died the previous year and that she had inherited the place from him.

"How about that." Mr. Selwyn smiled. "Well, it's a pleasure to meet you. Going to be staying the night?"

Jenny looked at Chaz. Unlike her, he seemed amenable. "Why not?"

"At least a few hours," Jenny said. Hopefully, not much more.

"Good. As it happens, I've got just the room available for you," Mr. Selwyn continued. "It's the one Gary and his lovely lady friend always used to occupy."

Jenny blinked. Sure she couldn't have heard right, she leaned toward him and repeated weakly, "His lady friend?"

"Sure," Mr Selwyn confirmed with a smile. Obviously having no idea how devastating this news was to Jenny, he continued informatively, "Every time Gary visited—and he visited oh, a couple times the past year—he always brought his lady friend with him. And they always requested the same room."

The same room. Gary. With another woman. Was there no end to his betrayal? Couldn't he have just stopped at throwing away her money? she wondered. Did he have to humiliate her this way, too?

Jenny felt her knees buckle as the sick feeling in the pit of her stomach expanded by leaps and bounds. Fortunately, Chaz's arm was there to steady her. He gave her a long, assessing survey. "Look, maybe that's not such a good idea," he intervened to Mr. Selwyn.

"Nonsense." Jenny cut in firmly, forcing herself to recover. "Of course I want to stay where my— where Gary and *his lady friend* stayed," she said. "Wh-what was her name again?"

"Lillian McCarry. She was a geologist, I think."

The same geologist Gary had gone caving with in
New Mexico, Jenny realized as the knife in her heart
twisted a little deeper.

"Say." Mr. Selwyn peered at her over the rim of
his bifocals. "Are you feeling all right?"

"No," Jenny said, fanning herself weakly as the
room began to spin. "I'm not. I—it must be the
heat. Maybe the...travel. Chaz?" she whispered, and
then the world went black.

"STAY DOWN, JENNY. Don't try to get up just yet."

Jenny moaned. As she shifted, the water bed
shifted beneath her. She blinked and blinked again
as a fuzzy image of herself slowly came into focus.
She turned weakly to Chaz. He was seated next to the
bed. In bone-colored trousers and a cadet blue shirt
that outlined every muscle on his chest, he had never
looked stronger or more ruggedly handsome. Despite everything, she was very glad he was there with
her. Even if she couldn't say the same for their surroundings. She looked above her once again and
blew out a chagrined breath. "Are those mirrors on
the ceiling, Chaz?"

He grinned in a way that let her know he was enjoying the frankly sexual nature of their surroundings much more than she. "'Fraid so," he replied.

"And what is *that*?" She pointed to a person-sized
wicker thingamajig suspended from the ceiling.

Chaz squinted at it. "I'm not sure. I think it's
some sort of chair swing," he speculated finally.

"Above a bed?"

"For people who're feeling somewhat creative?" he guessed.

Jenny moaned and covered her face with both hands. She didn't know what was more embarrassing, owning this place or actually being here. "I guess I don't have to ask where I am, do I?"

"Probably not," Chaz drawled as he stretched his long legs in front of him. "But just so you'll know, it's called the Amazon Room."

"How appropriate. And it was Gary's favorite," she continued bitterly. Tears stung her eyes, but she refused to let them fall. She'd been humiliated enough. "How could he have done that to me?" she asked miserably.

"I don't know." Chaz slipped onto the bed beside her and held tightly to her hand.

"He had an affair, Chaz."

He covered her hand with both of his, completely cosseting her hand with gentle warmth. The silence stretched between them endlessly. And yet Jenny felt comfort, just having him there with her. "We don't know that," Chaz said at length.

Even if Chaz was willing to give Gary the benefit of the doubt, Jenny refused to hide from the truth any longer. No matter how much it hurt, she had to face the facts. And she didn't want Chaz protecting her, either. "Don't we?" she retorted, hearing some of the irony creep back into her voice. "He died caving with that woman, Chaz." With her free hand, she rubbed at the tension gathering in her temples. "I'm so stupid, to have never once come even close to suspecting."

Chaz frowned. He dropped his hold on her hands and got up to prowl the room restlessly. "Maybe it's not what we think."

"Then why would he run around the country with that woman, and in secret? Why would they stay in this room together?" Jenny asked.

Chaz sighed. He glanced at her, looking briefly as deeply troubled as she felt. "I don't know. Maybe it had something to do with all that digging they were doing," he theorized finally.

"From what we've seen so far, I'd say she wasn't much of a geologist. Which leads me to wonder what her talents were."

"Jenny—"

Jenny pushed herself up, so she was seated against the headboard. "Don't say it, Chaz. Don't even try and defend him. I don't want to hear it, okay?"

His eyes held hers for a long, compassionate moment. He let out a long breath. "Okay."

Feeling abruptly as if she were on the verge of tears again, Jenny said in the most even voice she could muster, "I just want to be alone for a while."

Chaz didn't look as if he wanted to leave. Finally he nodded anyway. "Maybe that would be best," he said. He strode to the door, then paused with his hand on the knob. "I'll call you in a hour or so," he promised. "And we'll go to dinner."

ONLY THEY DIDN'T GO to dinner. They didn't go anywhere, mostly because Jenny wouldn't so much as answer his phone calls, Chaz thought grimly several hours later.

"Jenny, open up this door right now!" Chaz demanded. He was worried. It wasn't like her to cut herself off so completely. Generally, if she didn't want to do something, she simply told him to his face.

"Go away, Chaz!" Jenny's voice was a muffled sob on the other side of the locked door. "Just go away!"

Like hell he was going to go away when she was clearly in so much distress, Chaz thought, using the passkey he'd gotten from Mr. Selwyn to let himself in.

Jenny was sitting on the edge of the square-shaped bath for two. It was filled to the brim with bubbles. Clad in a short white terry-cloth robe, she had yet to get in the water. She sat straddling the edge of the tub, one foot dangling in the water, the other leg—and it was an enormously sexy leg, Chaz admitted to himself—propped on the top step of the stairs leading up to the tub. Her eyes were red and puffy. Her mass of golden hair had been swept on top of her head in a careless knot. She'd never looked sexier or more in need of a hug. It was all he could do to keep his distance and continue to give her space.

"I thought I told you to go away!" Jenny grumbled.

"You know me. I never could follow your directions." Chaz kicked off his shoes, strode up the steps and sank down on the opposite edge of the tub.

He dipped a hand in the bubbles and found them nice and warm. They smelled good, too, like the perfume Jenny habitually wore. "So what's going on?" he asked softly, trying not to notice the way the vee of her robe gaped open, revealing the curve of one creamy white breast.

"Nothing." Jenny stared at the bubbles.

"Why wouldn't you let me in?" he asked softly.

She shrugged. "I didn't feel like talking to anyone."

"Maybe you need to talk to someone."

She twisted both her hands in the hem of her robe and pressed the fabric down flat on the wide marble ledge between her thighs.

Jenny harrumphed. "Yeah, right, I think I'll just call all my best girlfriends back in Dallas and tell them I found out my husband not only ripped off my entire trust fund, but he was cheating on me, as well. Won't that be a hoot."

Turning in a semicircle away from him, she sank both her feet into the water and sat glumly facing the bathwater, dangling her legs over the edge of the tub, the way a kid dangles his feet in a stream.

Chaz kept one foot flat on the ledge. He propped his elbow on his upraised thigh and rested his chin on his palm. "So talk to me," he advised quietly as he continued to study her. "I already know everything anyway."

"No, Chaz. That's where you're wrong." Jenny's voice wavered emotionally and she got up abruptly, to wade to the opposite side of the tub. "You don't know everything about me."

Chaz got up and followed her across the tub. Jenny in a funk was a sight to behold. Her hair was a mess, yet it looked so soft and touchable he could barely keep himself from tunneling his hands through it and taking it down. Then again, he liked the way she had piled it up on the back of her head, because it left her delectable neck bare. Kissably bare.

Forcing himself to think about her problems, and not how desirable she looked with her cheeks all pink and her sable eyes dark with a mixture of desire and frustration, he sat beside her once again. "Like what don't I know about you?" he asked softly, hoping she'd trust him enough to really confide in him this time, and not just give him the bits and pieces of her life that she'd been doling out a morsel at a time.

Jenny swallowed hard, "Like the fact that I lied to you when I said I never knew anything about the property. I didn't know he'd bought property exactly, but I always suspected he was keeping something from me." Her voice caught again and she had to press her fist hard against her trembling lower lip before she could go on. Her eyes met his and held. "I was suspicious of the fact that he would disappear, sometimes out of reach by phone, and that he never invited me to go along with him to some of the activities, like caving.''

She shivered and hugged her arms against her chest as her words picked up speed, spilling out one after the other. ''He always told me I wouldn't like the things he did, that they were too rough and uncivilized for someone like me.'' She laughed, trying to mask her pain. She dodged Chaz's steady stare, looking instead at the pocket on his sport shirt. ''Little did I know that, when he wasn't home making passionate love with me, he was out there making passionate love with someone else.''

''Jenny,'' Chaz said, wishing she hadn't been married to his best friend. Wishing that the two of them could start fresh, with no history, no mistakes. And even though he knew he shouldn't want it, he wished he could kiss her again and make her forget her pain. Seeing her this way was worse than anything he had ever endured.

She shook her head in silent misery. ''He had an affair, Chaz!''

Chaz sighed. He wished he could bring back Gary, if only for the purpose of punching him in the nose for what he'd done to his wife. ''I know,'' he said sadly.

''No, you don't know!'' Jenny's voice caught and she stumbled to her feet, looking as if she'd just been hit with an avalanche of pain. Water splashed up past her knees. ''You can't possibly know how this hurts me. You can't possibly know how stupid and foolish and...and absolutely unlovable I feel at this very moment! What is wrong with me, Chaz, that Gary would feel he had to go to someone else?''

"There is absolutely nothing wrong with you, Jen, and you're not unlovable! You're the exact opposite," Chaz said. The next thing he knew he was standing in the tub next to her.

Her soft, bare lips compressed in silent misery. "Our relationship was so passionate, I thought that I'd never have to worry about Gary turning to another woman."

Chaz grasped her shoulders and held her in front of him. Angry not just at what Gary had done to his wife, but the way Jenny was berating herself, he continued sternly, "Gary was a fool if he stepped out on you, even once."

Standing face-to-face, her arms resting on his chest, she released a soft, sad sigh. "You may as well give up. Your pep talk is not going to work, Chaz."

Chaz had known for years that actions spoke louder than words. He placed a finger beneath her chin and tilted it back. His voice dropped another seductive notch as his eyes lovingly roved the pretty contours of her face. "Then what will work, Jenny?" he asked softly. Was it proof she needed? Did she want him to show her how desirable she really was? "Is this what you need?"

He hauled her against him, intending to kiss her just long enough to make his point. But something happened when his lips touched hers. Maybe it was magic, maybe it was something even more special, like love. Chaz didn't know. He only knew he'd never felt like this before, so open and free of heart. He'd never wanted so very much to please. And Jenny wanted to please him, too. He could feel it in the softness of her lips as they molded to his, in the tentative way her tongue touched his, in the way her hands left his chest, tunneled through his hair, and cupped his head above his ears, bringing him closer still.

Oh, yes, she wanted him, he thought. Wanted him and needed him. Now. Tonight.

Jenny hadn't expected this to happen. She was too confused to be thinking straight, and yet when Chaz touched her, when he held her and kissed her, her world suddenly righted itself. In Chaz's arms, she felt safe, secure. In his kiss, she felt tenderness, desire and the blooming of something else... something very special.

Dizzied by the feelings whirling in her heart, she weakened at the knees and sagged against him. He caught her to him, hard. Her robe rose up. His hand connected with the silkiness of her hips and he dis-covered what he had already suspected—that she was naked beneath it. Chaz groaned and deepened the kiss. Too far gone to think about the wisdom of anything, Jenny touched her tongue to his, wrapped her arms about his neck and lifted one leg, wrap-ping it intimately around his thigh. Passion thrummed through her, white-hot and intense. Jenny moaned, caught up in the possibilities. She wanted him inside her, against her, skin to skin, starting at the juncture of their bodies. She ran her hands over his strong shoulders, bringing him even closer.

The next thing Chaz knew, he was staggering backward. The two of them were waist deep in bubbles. Jenny was curled up inside his spread thighs. And still she kissed him as if her life depended on it. And maybe, he thought as he kissed her back just as raptly, it did. She needed this. Needed him.

"Oh, Chaz," Jenny whispered lovingly as she pressed tiny kisses down his neck. And suddenly Chaz knew, if he made love to her now, when she was still on the rebound from Gary, still hurting, that she would resent him again.

I can't do this, he thought, even as she opened her robe and placed his hand inside. I can't take advantage of her, he thought as his palm cupped the warmth of her breast, rubbed the tip into rosy awareness, and moved sideways to explore the other. But it didn't feel as though he were taking advantage, Chaz thought as she moved restlessly beneath him and found his mouth once again. Not even when his hand dropped lower, ghosting across her abdomen, lower still, finding the juncture of her thighs.

Wanting her to see how much he cared about her, how much he wanted to please her, he caressed her intimately, taking his cues from the way her body reacted, deepening the caress when she arched against him, repeating it when she moaned. She shuddered and collapsed against him. For several moments longer, her movements continued to be jerky. He furthered her pleasure as best he could, then held her close, wrapping her in his arms and pressing her tight against him.

Finally Jenny opened her eyes. She looked dazed and a little in awe. Her hand drifted lower, to the hard ridge of arousal in his pants. She caressed him wonderingly. "You didn't..."

"No," Chaz said gruffly, not so sure the decision he'd made earlier, when they'd started to kiss, had been the right one. But he was determined to stick with it, for both their sakes. "And I'm not going to," he confessed heavily as he let out a long, uneven breath. "Not tonight. Not now, Jenny." His eyes caressed her tearstained face tenderly. "Not when you're so obviously distressed."

Her mouth dropped open in a round O of surprise. The pleasure-induced flush on her face turned an alabaster white, then a dark red. She grasped the edges of her robe together and shoved away from him. "You just had to do that, didn't you?" she stormed.

"Do what?" Chaz said. All he'd been trying to do was protect her, and save her from any more hurt.

Jenny got up on trembling legs, her short, skimpy robe clinging damply about her. "Humiliate me!" she stormed.

Humiliate her! Chaz surged to his feet. "I did no such thing," he defended himself quickly.

"Oh, really. You just made me react to you. And for what? So you could see for yourself how easy it is for you to seduce me?"

"It wasn't like that at all," he countered roughly. He had kissed and touched her because she'd needed to be loved. Because he'd wanted her to feel loved. And because he'd wanted to give her pleasure. Since when was that a crime? Since now, he decided, looking at the accusing look on her face.

He waded through the dwindling bubbles. She moved out of the tub, trying to avoid him. He moved with her, his motions as sure and slow as hers were jerky and confused. Water splashed out in rivulets on the tile floor as he stepped down beside her and hauled her back into his arms, drenched robe and all. "Jenny, listen to me. I was not trying to humiliate you," he explained patiently as he searched the depths of her sable brown eyes, which looked even darker and more luminous when rimmed with tears. "I was trying to show you what a desirable woman you are."

She wanted to believe him. He could tell. But her past with Gary made it hard for her to do so.

Jenny inhaled a trembling breath as her eyes held his. "But not desirable enough for you to want to make love to," she accused.

Damn, but she was beautiful with her lashes all wet and spiky, her lips bare and slightly swollen from their kisses, her golden hair falling down around her shoulders. So beautiful he...no. He couldn't let himself get sidetracked again. He had to show her how he felt, even if he had to be crude to do so.

Chaz grasped her hand and forced it down, to the apex of his thighs. Curling her resisting fingers around his throbbing manhood, it was all he could do not to groan. "Does that feel like someone who doesn't want you?" he rasped out. His eyes bored into hers, further accentuating his words. "I ache for you, Jenny. But I'm not going to do anything about it," he said hoarsely. He tore her hand away and placed it between them, positioning it so it lay flat against his chest. "Because that wouldn't be fair. Not tonight. Not after all you've been through."

"Then why did you—" Jenny's lower lip trembled. She evidently found it difficult to go on. "Why did you touch me like that?" she whispered hoarsely.

"Because—oh hell, I don't know why I did what I did," Chaz swore. "Except maybe I wanted you to have some release. And maybe...maybe I couldn't help myself. I want to touch you, Jenny," he confided softly. He'd never spoken so intimately or freely with any woman. "I want to touch you all the time. If you don't know that—"

Jenny's eyes were huge in her pale face. She was silent, unsure, and far too vulnerable for him to have kissed tonight. Chaz swallowed hard. "So I'm guilty as charged," he continued, only telling her what he already saw was in her heart, and in the heart of every golden girl he had ever started to care about. The knowledge he wasn't good enough for her. Not now. Not ever.

". . . THEY STARTED DIGGING last year," Mr. Selwyn told Chaz and Jenny early the following morning.

"Why?" Jenny asked. To her relief, Chaz was acting as if nothing out of the ordinary had happened between them.

Mr. Selwyn shrugged. "Started out as something wrong with the septic tank. We don't have full city services this far out of Las Vegas, you know. Pumped in water and electricity and that's about all. Anyway, like I said, they were digging around, something to do with the septic tank, and then Gary's lady friend showed up and started supervising, too. Anyway, she inspected everything, even climbed down herself in those big holes they dug a couple of times."

"Did she take any samples?" Jenny asked, more sure than ever that the methodical Gary had been on to something. If only they could discover what!

"Can't rightly say about that, miss. I didn't get so close to it myself. I don't really like to mess with them septic tanks, seeing as they contain chemicals and all. Anyway, pretty soon they fixed it all up—not that I ever noticed there was anything wrong with it in the first place—and that's the last was done for it, or anything else around here."

Mr. Selwyn shrugged. "I tried to talk to him once about redecorating...some of the themed rooms are getting pretty stale, if you know what I mean, and I felt a new idea or two might help boost business. Not that our hourly business is all that bad, you understand, but we're just not getting much of the honeymoon crowd. But I was thinking..."

Jenny let Mr. Selwyn ramble on, too embarrassed to interrupt. Besides, Chaz looked interested in everything Mr. Selwyn had to say, Jenny noticed as she absently turned to study the postcard rack next to the front desk.

Thinking back on it, she couldn't believe what had happened yesterday. Chaz breaking into her room, yes. In retrospect, she was only surprised he hadn't done that sooner. She could also believe he'd given her a pep talk. What else was he supposed to do, when she was crying her eyes out and making an absolute fool of herself? The kiss...again, maybe.

But there her expectations had stopped. He had held her and touched her and kissed her as if he had every intention of making love to her. And she had gloried in the feeling, in the wanton abandonment he inspired in her. In Chaz's arms, she felt like a very sexy woman. In Chaz's arms, she felt thoroughly loved. And that she hadn't expected.

Because she knew even if she wanted to, she could not allow herself to fall in love with Chaz. He wasn't her type. They had nothing in common, save their past link to Gary.

A love affair between them would never work, even short term. So why couldn't she get the idea out of her mind? Why couldn't she get rid of this nagging feeling that she was doing the stupidest thing of all, even as they stood here listening to Mr. Selwyn ramble on. That she was falling in love with Chaz. Deeply, irrevocably in love.

"ELEVEN MILLION IS a tremendous amount of money, Dr. McCarry."

"As I've told you, I will pay that back, with interest, within the year. As soon as I get my new business up and running."

"It's still a lot of money."

Lillian looked the banker straight in the eye. "The land is worth it and you know it," she said quietly. "Not to mention the fact that you're in this with me from the ground floor up. As a start-up investor, you'll eventually stand to make millions, too."

The Atlanta banker's eyes gleamed avariciously as he tapped his pencil against the edge of his polished teak desk. "Does this mean you've convinced Mrs. Olson to sell her properties to you?"

Lillian sat up a little straighter in her chair, wishing for the hundredth time that Gary were still with her, handling the financial end of things. She preferred to handle just the geological end. "Not yet," she admitted, albeit reluctantly, thinking of the single bid Jenny had already rejected for the Colorado property. "But I will."

The bank president tipped his swivel chair back and waited to be convinced. "How?"

Lillian thought about the unpaid taxes on all the properties, and the bills that Jenny would soon be getting on each of them. Jenny Olson was a person with tremendous wealth and style, a person with a top-notch credit rating. If she could have afforded to keep her properties up and pay the taxes on all of them, she would have done so. Which only meant one thing. Gary had stretched her trust fund as far as it would go, and now she was in a position where she either had to sell—or go bust.

"She'll sell to me," Lillian said with quiet confidence. *As long as she doesn't know it's me, the woman who was with Gary when he died, that she's dealing with.* "All she really cares about is getting her trust fund back. The immediate sale of her properties to my new company Properties, Inc., plus the profit I have built into the sale, will allow her to recoup her losses and go on with her life, as she should have all along."

"And if she doesn't see it that way? What then?"

A tiny film of perspiration beaded Lillian's upper lip and bathed her underarms. She couldn't make it this far and not succeed. She had sacrificed too much, worked too hard. "Jenny Olson will sell," Lillian repeated firmly. *And then we'll both profit handsomely, just as Gary wanted.*

Chapter Eleven

"What do you mean there's no road to the plantation?" Chaz asked as Jenny parked the rental car with Louisiana plates next to a fish and bait shop along the Atchafalaya River.

Looking like a belle at a tea party in a frilly white dress, she stepped from the car and said, "It's being torn up to make way for the new freeway that's being built between Baton Rouge and Alexandria."

Chaz tore his eyes from the layers of sheer white fabric hugging her breasts and watched as she tugged on lacy white gloves and angled a broad white hat jauntily over her forehead. Damned if she didn't look as pretty as a bride on her wedding day, he thought. "So how are we supposed to get to this plantation?" Chaz asked.

"I rented a powerboat to get us through the swamp," she said, then waved at the young kid in the Dufrene's Bait Shop T-shirt heading their way.

"Where, once we arrive, we'll be greeted with mint juleps and huge slices of Mississippi mud pie," Chaz supposed dryly, then frowned at the way the teenage boy was ogling Jenny.

Jenny blew out a breath. "Don't be ridiculous. There's no full-time house staff living or working at the plantation now."

"Then why are you wearing that getup?" Chaz asked impatiently. *Unless it's to give me a hard-on that won't quit?* He jerked a handkerchief out of his hip pocket, dabbed at the moisture on his brow and tried not to look at the way the full skirt on her dress swirled sexily down to midcalf. Which was, he figured moments later, pretty much a lost cause. Like heat-seeking missiles on a target, his eyes kept roving her voluptuous figure again and again.

"Because you never know who you'll run into," Jenny said. *Who knew how much longer she would be able to afford to buy beautiful clothes? She might as well wear what she had as long as she could.* Because Chaz was still looking at her quizzically, she said, "I'm wearing a dress because that's what all Southern ladies wear."

Southern ladies or society ladies? Chaz wondered, but didn't say. "Even in the swamp?" he chided.

Although he'd expected this trip to bring them closer together and somehow alleviate the differences between them, it had only served to point them out more accurately. The truth was, Jenny was more of a golden girl than ever, more his fantasy, more out of reach. What did it matter if he was in love with her—and Chaz was willing to admit that he was in love with her. Deeply, irrevocably in love.

"We're not wading through the swamp." Jenny studied the back seat of the car, then brought out a lacy white parasol that matched her dress. "We are riding through it."

Chaz followed her and the kid over to the pier next to the bait shop. "Have you ever been in a swamp?"

Jenny turned, in a drift of perfume. "No," she admitted uncomfortably.

"Then that makes two of us," Chaz said.

"But I've always wanted to own a Southern plantation," Jenny said as she signed the papers the boy held out, paid him fifty dollars of her dwindling cash and accepted her copy of the receipt. "Now I'll finally have my chance."

Chance to get back at him was more like it, Chaz thought as the three of them tromped down to the end of the dock, where an aluminum rowboat with a power motor attached to one end of it bobbed in the murky green water.

He was sure she hadn't forgiven him for starting to make love to her and then stopping. She still felt he had done it to hurt her, rather than to keep her from being hurt while he was still aching with a need not even a thousand bone-chilling cold showers could erase. No, the only thing that was going to soothe him was to bury himself so deep inside her...he had to stop thinking like this. Thinking like this was what had gotten him in trouble in the first place.

"I'll sit in the back next to the motor," Chaz said when the boy bent to begin untying the rope.

Jenny shook her head imperiously. "I'm driving."

"Steering, you mean," Chaz corrected, "and, no, you're not, either."

Slapping her closed parasol against her palm, she whirled to face him. "Need I remind you who paid for the use of this boat?"

Chaz reached for his wallet. "Do you want me to pay for half?" He was more than willing. It was Jenny who got uptight at any reminder of how broke she was.

Jenny snapped open her parasol and held it up to the sun. "No, I do not want you to subsidize this trip," Jenny said stiffly. "If I've told you once, I've told you a hundred times, this is my problem, and I will handle it. I simply want you to stop being so crabby."

Then you stop looking so damned beautiful, he thought. Stop twirling that damned parasol around and wearing your hair all loose and soft and free. Stop wearing clothes that hug your body and play up your femininity to the hilt. Stop making me think of how much I want to make love to you, slowly, every waking minute of the night and day.

"Let's get something straight," Chaz said, glaring down at her. "There is no way you're steering this boat, Jenny. Particularly when you're messing with some damned parasol at the same time.''

"Fine.'' She shrugged her shoulders indifferently. "Then there's no way you're going with me. You'll just have to try to find your own boat. And since I've got the only copy of the map..."

The kid in the bait shop T-shirt and bill cap grinned. "She's got you there, buddy."

Chaz gave him a long, level look. "You really want this nut manning your outboard, fella? Particularly since she's never so much as paddled a canoe in her life before today?"

The kid whitened.

Jenny sent Chaz a withering glare. She turned on the thousand-watt charm as she smiled at the young kid. "I have insurance, honey. Lots and lots of it. If I ruin your boat you'll get a brand-new one and you won't have to pay a thing."

The kid in the bill cap smiled at Jenny and shrugged at Chaz. "The lady steers the boat. Sorry, mister."

"You heard our host," Jenny said, climbing with some difficulty into the back of the boat. It rocked back and forth as she attempted to balance her weight. Twice she almost upset it entirely. Finally she was settled at the rear of the boat. Chaz climbed wearily in the front. "If we go overboard we're both gonna get covered with leeches," he said.

Jenny whitened, but her chin went up. She stared at him defiantly, letting him know with that one glance that nothing and no one intimidated her any longer. "If it happens, it happens," she said flatly. "Now, how do I start this thing?"

"WE'RE LOST."

"Are not."

"Are, too."

Chaz released a long-suffering breath that grated on Jenny's nerves like fingernails on a chalkboard. "Let me look at the map, Jenny."

"Fine," she snapped back, tired of being underestimated and undermined by him at every turn. Tired of being the woman he felt sorry for. "Look at it! It's not going to tell you anything more than it's telling me." Her temper flaring up and out of control, she tossed the map at him. The wind sprang up the moment the flimsy paper went airborne. Chaz leaped up to catch it, almost unseating them both, before he sat back down carefully on the middle bench.

Jenny's heart was pounding as she realized how close they had come to taking a dunking in the murky waters of the swamp. Determined not to show him how much she hated the rugged, outdoorsy parts of their adventure, she carefully maintained her regal bearing. "Nice catch," Jenny complimented him insouciantly, though her hands were still clutching the aluminum sides of the boat.

Chaz looked up, then nodded past her shoulder. "Nice alligator."

Jenny blinked, sure she hadn't heard right. "What?"

"I said, 'Nice alligator,'" Chaz responded as his sea blue eyes took on a challenging glint. "It's swimming along behind us."

Jenny shot him a droll look and rolled her eyes. "Very funny, Chaz," she said as she turned around. He was always trying to scare her. Trying to make her think she needed him along, to protect her from potential rock slides in abandoned silver mines and . . . oh, my God.

Her heart stopped. Nosing along behind them, its snout level with the gray-green water, was an alligator. True, it wasn't much of one by alligator standards—this one was only a foot or two long—but it was still an alligator, big teeth and all.

Jenny didn't stop to think. She just reacted and dived for Chaz's lap. Only the fact he was firmly braced in the middle of the rowboat kept them both from flying into the murky water. She clung to his waist. When she could speak again, she muttered something wholly unladylike.

Chaz continued to study the map, one arm tightly anchored around her waist. "I think you're right," he said slowly, holding her close. Though Jenny had never put much stock in male protection, never really felt she needed any before, she had a new appreciation for the concept. When it came to crawly, scaly, dangerous things, maybe it wouldn't be so bad to have a man in her life.

"I think we are going in the right direction," Chaz continued absently, as Jenny's heartbeat slowed and she became aware of the fresh clean scent of his skin and the brisk, sun-warmed scent of his cologne. And the tantalizingly sexual memories both evoked. "At least we will be—" Chaz smiled and put Jenny aside and headed for the back "—if someone steers this craft."

He powered the boat much faster than Jenny did, she noted, still shaking a little as they put the alligator far behind. So fast that twenty minutes later they were at the edge of the swamp. A wooden pier some fifty feet in length extended between the edge of the water and the high ground the house was on.

"So this is the place," Chaz said.

Jenny looked at the imposing plantation house, thought of the nearly six million dollars in cash Gary had reportedly paid for this place, and felt her heart sink. She'd thought the two million he'd paid in Colorado, the .7 million in Idaho, and the 1.3 million in Nevada had been bad investments. But *this* was a fiscal nightmare.

Not that the imposing plantation home wasn't nice. The two-story Grecian mansion made out of white brick was very impressive. It had burgundy shutters and two levels of wraparound verandas, and looked well kept. But from what she'd just seen, most of the two hundred plus acres of land comprising the Whispering Oaks plantation was swampland, on the east side of the Atchafalaya River. It was out in the middle of nowhere. There was simply no way it was worth what Gary had paid for it.

Realizing that, she wanted to give up, but she knew she couldn't. This was the last property Gary had purchased, her last chance to make sense of what he'd done. She tossed the rope to the wooden post at the end of the pier and anchored the boat. "Let's go on up and have a look around."

"I'll bring the map," Chaz said. He fell into step beside her, shortening his strides to accommodate her smaller ones. Jenny tried not to think how nice it was simply to be with Chaz. Or how much she had come to rely on seeing him every day. She would miss him when they returned home to Dallas.

And yet she knew, even as she realized she was falling in love with him, that a relationship with him would never work, long term. Chaz wasn't interested in settling down. And she wasn't interested in a man who cared primarily about the specifics of his next adventure.

"So, how much of the land Gary bought is under water?" Chaz asked.

"According to the map, nearly half of it," Jenny said with a frown. She looked up at Chaz from beneath the brim of her lacy white sun hat. "But I guess that would depend on how much rainfall they have, and would vary from year to year. You can see the watermarks on some of the trees in the swamps."

"So at one point the water was even higher than it was today," Chaz surmised.

"Right."

"And probably as summer wanes and the heat increases, it will get even dryer."

"Right," Jenny said, relieved, "and the water level will go down."

"Is that the road crew in the distance?" Chaz asked.

Jenny followed his gaze. "Certainly looks like it," she said, perking up just a little. "Let's go talk to them and see what they know."

"Sounds good to me."

As they neared the bulldozers where the workers were taking a break, Jenny lifted her hand in a vibrant wave and called cheerfully to the men in the bright orange construction vests, "Hello there!"

Chaz was beginning to see where that dress, and the way Jenny looked in it, might come in handy. Maybe wearing it hadn't been such a dumb move on her part after all. Certainly, it had to be hard to say no to her when she looked the way she did. Ten to one, the men would want to chat it up with Jenny as long as possible....

The men smiled at her, and she swiftly made introductions, lamented with the men on the hot, humid Louisiana weather, talked about the road some, and how much easier it would be to get to the house once it was finished, then finally got down to what she really wanted to know. "So, how long have you been working on this road?" Jenny asked.

"About fifteen months or so," the road crew boss, a burly man in his fifties named Pete Johnson, said.

"Did you ever meet my husband, Gary?"

There was some restless shifting among the men. "Yes, ma'am. We met him, all right," Pete answered. "He was always underfoot when he was in the area."

"What do you mean?""

"Well—" Pete took off his helmet and ran his hand through his burr haircut "—he was mighty interested in the rumors about the dig."

"Dig?" Jenny and Chaz perked up simultaneously. They exchanged an excited glance.

Pete shrugged. "Some scientist from LSU swears there are dinosaur bones buried out here. Says he saw an entire skeleton in the swamp three years ago. Before he could get the bones out, it started to rain. One of them tropical storms. Water level rose. When he went back later, assuming he went to the right place, he couldn't find any trace of what he'd seen."

"He must have been heartbroken," Jenny murmured, her mind racing ahead.

"Not to mention humiliated," Pete Johnson agreed. "Is that what y'all are doing down here? Looking for them dinosaur bones, too?"

"I take it we're not the first," Chaz said.

"Nope. Course, no one's ever found nothin', neither. So you're probably wasting your time, if you're here to look."

Jenny didn't think so. "I need to look at the property, too," she said pleasantly, "and decide what to do about the house." She shook hands with one and all, concluding the interview. "Thank you. You've been most helpful."

They were a short distance away before she spoke again. "It was nice of you to let me handle that."

"No reason not to." Chaz shrugged as he once again adjusted his steps to hers. "You were doing a great job investigating."

Jenny was silent a moment, thinking. "Do you think that's what Gary's been after, too? Dinosaur bones?"

Chaz shrugged and put a hand to the small of her back as they walked the long, gravel-lined driveway to the house. "It would make sense, wouldn't it?" he said, sparing a glance for the rows of towering oaks on either side of them. "Dinosaur bones are not only very rare, they're worth a great deal of money. And if he was digging everywhere he bought—the silver mine in Colorado, the well in Idaho, around the septic lines in Vegas—"

"He wasn't digging here," Jenny interrupted, enjoying their brainstorming. "At least not according to any information I have."

"How do we know that? He might have been digging like crazy and just not put anything on paper about it. Or brought back any papers to Dallas. We know for sure he was interested in the ground the road crews tore up."

"True." Jenny paused, looking at the house. "It's going to be dark in three or four hours," she said.

"What do you want to do? Hitch a ride with the road crews and head back to town that way or stay out here for the night?"

Jenny didn't relish the thought of being alone with Chaz in the big, empty plantation home, but she also knew they needed to be here if they were to make the most of the time they had to explore the grounds and house. "Let's spend the night out here. But first, I've got a phone call to make."

"I BROUGHT THE THINGS you asked for, Ms. Olson, including all your luggage, the groceries, and the four-wheel-drive Jeep," the teenager from Dufrene's Bait Shop said.

Jenny stepped out onto the veranda. The Jeep he'd brought her looked as if it had been through World War II and still had some of the original mud on it. But it was also exactly what they needed to be able to get around the torn-up roads leading to the plantation house, and the plantation grounds themselves. "Thank you." She went through the ritual of signing rental agreements, then paid him.

Pocketing the money, he asked, "You're sure you're not going to need the boat anymore?"

Jenny glanced at the river and thought of the alligator they'd seen, and knew she'd explored enough of the swampy waters for right now. "Not in the next day or so," she said, "but if we find out otherwise, I'll call you."

The teenage boy looked eager to stay round. "Want me to help you carry in the groceries and the luggage?"

"We can handle it," Chaz said proprietorially, stepping out to join her. For a second, Jenny wondered if he could be jealous of the boy's obvious attraction to her, then decided the thought was crazy and pushed it aside. Chaz was just being his usual take-charge self, she reassured herself firmly. If he looked irritated, it was by the number of suitcases she'd brought and nothing else.

Briefly the boy looked disappointed. "Well then, I better get back to the bait shop 'fore it gets too dark to see my way back upriver."

"Thanks again." Jenny smiled at him.

Chaz and Jenny were silent as they carried in the bags of groceries from the back of the Jeep. "You're very quiet," she said as she lifted the milk and juice from the cooler and put them in the plantation house refrigerator.

Chaz lifted out clear cellophane bags of fresh fruits and vegetables. "I was just thinking how much you've changed in the last couple of weeks."

Jenny warmed at the compliment she heard in his voice, but, recalling the inherent differences between them, cautioned herself not to make too much of it. He was probably just being nice to make up for the grumpy way he'd been behaving this morning.

"What do you mean?" She looked up at him and saw their time boating downriver had left the glow of sunburn on his face.

"Well, look at you. You've been running around all day. Running all over the country, to be specific," he amended, "and yet you're not the least bit worn-out."

"Oh, I'm tired all right," Jenny said with a sigh, oddly touched by his concern for her welfare. "But driven, too," she continued. "I've got to find out why Gary wanted these properties, Chaz. Not to mention why he went to such lengths to keep them secret from me." She put a box of whole-grain cereal on the counter with a thud, then turned around to face him. "So far, the dinosaur bones theory sounds the most promising. But there are other reasons he might have wanted the properties, too."

"Such as?" Chaz prodded.

"Well, all the areas we've looked at have value as potential resorts."

"Except the Colorado location is too remote, and the potato farm awfully flat."

Jenny leaned against the counter and crossed her arms casually at her waist. "Lakes can be man-made. Roads can be built. Maybe he knew something we don't."

"Such as?"

Jenny shrugged, hoping she wasn't going to look like a fool later for sharing her half-formed ideas with Chaz now. "Maybe a new resort area was being planned in each of these places. Maybe Gary was the person making the plans."

"Then why the geological surveys?" Chaz asked.

"I don't know. That kind of goes back to the dinosaur bones theory, doesn't it?"

Chaz's blue eyes darkened thoughtfully. "Or something else valuable. Like oil or coal or—"

Jenny sighed and held up a hand to cut him off. "I've already researched that thoroughly, Chaz. With the exception of the small amounts of silver that originally were found in the Colorado mine, none of the areas were remotely connected to any valuable mineral or resource."

"Which leaves us back at square one," Chaz theorized dismally.

"The dinosaur bones." They both fell silent. In the quiet, dark cool of the huge plantation kitchen, Jenny couldn't help but think about what it would be like to kiss him here. In the understated elegance of the rambling house. Telling herself she was only torturing herself by thinking such things, Jenny turned her mind back to the business at hand.

"Maybe he did know something we don't," she suggested hopefully, then flushed at the unexpected intensity in his eyes.

Chaz sighed, the intimacy in his look fading as quickly as it had appeared, leaving her feeling even more bereft. She wanted to be friends with Chaz. She wanted to be more than friends. She just didn't know if it would ever be possible. And yet, a small idealistic part of her couldn't let go of the hope...any more than she could let go of the memories of his kisses....

Chaz stepped back, away from her. "For your sake, I hope he did, Jenny," he said. "This place is nice. In fact, I don't think I've ever walked through a nicer plantation home." Jenny knew what he meant. With its collection of freshly painted walls, Aubusson rugs, and lovingly cared for antiques, the house was both warm and wonderful. But it wasn't worth millions. She doubted, given its location, she could even sell it for two million.

Jenny sighed. What had Gary been thinking?

Chapter Twelve

"Stay on the road, Jenny."

Hearing the highly irascible note in his low, sexy tone, Jenny tightened her hands on the steering wheel of the ancient Jeep and defiantly stayed her course. "We can't see anything from here, Chaz," she countered, her soft voice as amiable as his was gruff.

"We can see enough," Chaz argued, turning to face her. He propped the flat of one hand against the rusted-out dash as the warm summer wind tossed his hair into soft chestnut spikes. "If we leave the road, we're liable to get stuck in the mud."

Jenny wished he'd take off his mirrored aviator sunglasses so she could see the expression in his sea blue eyes, although she supposed, the unamused set of his sensual mouth was clue enough as to how he was feeling about being the follower, instead of the leader, in this latest episode of her adventure. Well, too bad, she thought. She had given up control of her life, albeit unknowingly, when she was married to Gary. She wasn't going to make the same mistake again. It was her turn now to not only control her own destiny and her finances, but to set things right, and she damn well was going to take it.

Turning her eyes back to the road in front of her, Jenny argued her point calmly, "There's no mud out there, Chaz. Dirt, yeah, plenty of it, but mud, no."

Chaz inhaled deeply and then pushed a stream of air out through his teeth. "Looks can be deceiving, Jenny."

Yes, Jenny thought wistfully, she knew that very well. For instance, she'd thought more than once during this trip that Chaz was beginning to fall in love with her, only to see later that he didn't love her at all, but merely felt sorry for her because of the situation Gary had put her in. No doubt he'd be only too happy to get rid of her once this trip had ended. And he would probably expedite that process by fixing her up with Mr. Right, as he had promised.

There weren't any words to express the depth of misery she felt at that prospect. It was bad enough to know she meant no more than any of the other women he'd helped through a bad time. But to see how easily he could move on without her. To know she was just another damsel in distress . . . Jenny gulped. That was too much to be borne.

Chaz bit down on an expletive as she steered the Jeep abruptly to the right and they left the gravel lane circling the parts of the plantation grounds that were above water. "I hope we don't live to regret this." He pushed the words through his teeth.

Jenny rolled her eyes as they bounced roughly over the uneven terrain. "Will you relax?" she said as her bottom bumped up and down on the weathered leather seat. "I know what I'm doing. I took four-wheel driving lessons from a Jeep dealership in Dallas before we left ... oh, my word!" Jenny braked sharply and rose as far up out of her seat as her shoulder belt would allow. Peering over the steering wheel, she studied a huge jagged-edged crater. Nowhere near where they were building the highway, it looked nonetheless as if it had been dug out by a steam shovel. "Would you look at that, Chaz?" she crowed excitedly. "We found where Gary was digging!"

She cut the motor, unfastened her lap belt and vaulted from the Jeep in one smooth motion. Chaz bounded after her.

"Careful, Jenny!" he warned as she trod fearlessly toward the edge.

Too late, her shoes were already sticking like glue to the oozing dark brown earth. With considerable effort, she lifted one foot out of the muck, then the other. Each subsequent step she took made dark, squishy sounds. Nearby, Chaz was striding forward on solid ground that was apparently as dry as hers was wet.

Feeling like a fool but determined not to let this little glitch in her adventure bring her down, Jenny

marched in slow-motion, suction-cup agony over to
the grassy slope where he was standing. Once on the
grass, she rested a hand on his forearm for balance
and busied herself wiping the mud—or as much of it
as she could—off her shoes. "How did you know it
was wet over there?" she asked.

Chaz shrugged. "Just a guess."

Not that it had taken a genius to know unvege-
tated terrain in a marshland would be pure mud, he
thought. Just as it hadn't taken a genius to realize
that each day he was with Jenny would be more and
more difficult. Not that she was making their trip
together unpleasant. With the exception of her mule-
headedness about solving her problems single-
handedly, she was very nice to be around. Very nice
to look at, too, Chaz thought, his glance trailing
down over her increasingly slender form. Today she
had on some sort of safari getup that she'd probably bought at Banana Republic. Khaki shirt, knee-
length khaki shorts, bone-colored knee socks and
ankle-high hiking boots that were covered with mud.
The only things missing from her getup were a can-
teen to strap across her chest and a helmet. And he
was willing to bet she had both items locked away in
one of her half dozen suitcases.

In any other woman, her penchant for beautiful,
sometimes ridiculous, clothes would have been an-
noying to him. Generally he had no patience for the
kind of women who had to dress for every occasion,
no matter how inane. In Jenny, the trait was endear-

ing, and as much a part of her as his own need to breathe. Maybe because that was how she had been brought up, as a golden girl who had everything her heart desired. A golden girl who needed a similarly brought up golden boy.

Unaware of the way he was unabashedly ogling her behind the protection of his sunglasses, Jenny peered into the hole. "What's down there?"

"Beats me." Chaz looked down into the empty crater, where a shallow pool of water glinted in the hot Louisiana sunshine. He shrugged. Telling himself it was to keep Jenny from tumbling in, head over heels, he draped a protective arm about her shoulders. "I see rock and dirt."

"But no bones." Jenny frowned.

"No bones, silver or gold," he specified. This close to her, he could smell her perfume and see a faint spot of moisture on her blouse, and know that moisture was beginning to gather between her breasts. He wondered how she would look, were they to make love in this climate, her naked body glistening wetly with the heat. Then he pushed the thought away. It was the unguarded moments like this, the times when he began to fantasize about what could be between them, that were the most dangerous.

"Well, at least we know Gary was digging here, too." Taking comfort in that fact, Jenny slid her hands into the pockets of her shorts and headed back for the Jeep.

Behind her, Chaz noticed the way the action drew the soft cotton fabric even tighter across her hips. Blood surged in his lower half and it was all he could do not to groan out loud.

"Now if we only knew why," Chaz said grimly, the unhappy note in his voice more due to the erection that swelled and strained against the front of his jeans than his worry over what Gary had done and why.

To him, the past was just that. And though he could wring Gary's neck for the misery he'd put Jenny through, it was the future Chaz was really worried about. Would he really be able to fix Jenny up with some blue-blooded Mr. Right, as he had promised?

"We have to face it," Jenny said over her shoulder. "We may never...oh, my gosh. Chaz, look!" Jenny knelt in the grass.

"Corings," Chaz murmured, picking up one of the long cylinder-shaped rods that were all of the same size—nearly three feet in length and three inches in diameter.

"What?"

Chaz handed Jenny one of the heavy rods. "These are geological samples. Someone has been drilling here, Jenny."

"One...two...Chaz, there are eight of these rods here!"

"Looks like someone either forgot them or had to leave in a hurry."

"Or they're worthless," Jenny speculated, "and were left behind for that reason."

"There's only one way to find out." Chaz picked up six of the heavy corings and let Jenny carry two. "We'll take them back to Dallas and have them analyzed."

"That'll cost money, Chaz. A lot of money." Jenny bit her lip. "I barely have enough money to get back to Dallas as it is."

Chaz shrugged. "So I'll spot you the cash you need and you can pay me back later."

Jenny paused and lifted the dark gray corings in her arms. "You'd do that for me?"

And a far sight more, Chaz thought. Aware how sensitive Jenny was about being broke, he shrugged. "Sure, why not?"

Jenny continued to study him relentlessly. "Given my circumstances, it might take me a while to pay you back."

"I'm a patient man, Jen." Chaz dumped the corings into the back of the Jeep.

"So I've noticed. Thank you, Chaz." She paused. "I appreciate the offer."

"Even if you won't take me up on it?"

Jenny's grin was rueful. Her golden hair streaming over her shoulders, Jenny climbed behind the wheel and belted herself in. Finally she turned to him, her sable eyes earnest. "Maybe we'll find another place, more corings, if we just keep looking."

"Maybe," Chaz allowed, but he didn't feel nearly as hopeful as she obviously did. In his opinion, they were incredibly lucky to have gotten what they had. Smiling in her anticipation, Jenny turned the key, put the Jeep into gear and gave them an unhappy surprise.

"IT IS NOT MY FAULT we got stuck in the mud!" Jenny declared long moments later.

The blouse that had been damp was now soaked with perspiration, as was evidently her camisole, Chaz noted. He could see the imprint of her nipples clearly through the damp, clinging cloth. Feeling as though the whole lower half of him was on fire, Chaz shifted the corings in his arms—because of the distance they had to walk, he had volunteered to carry all eight—and advised, "Just keep walking, Jen."

Jenny didn't know why he was being so rude about all this. Only that he was getting grumpier with every second that passed. If only he'd take off those damn sunglasses, she thought, so she could see his eyes, then maybe she'd know how to handle him, what to say. "If we'd had a rug, a bag of sand, something," she theorized.

"We still couldn't have gotten it out," Chaz said gruffly. "The wheels are in way too deep," he finished.

"I said I was sorry," she whispered.

"I know you did," Chaz acknowledged curtly, picking up the pace of their trek a little more.

Jenny had to struggle to catch up with him. Irritated with him for the way he was behaving, irritated with herself for allowing him to get to her, she closed a hand over his bicep. "So?"

Chaz skidded to a halt and turned to face her. The arresting planes of his face—the high cheekbones, the straight nose, the sensually chiseled mouth—looked even more handsome because of his tenseness. "So you're sorry and we're stuck walking back to the plantation house on foot," he said.

Jenny knew, even though he hadn't come right out and said so, that she was the cause of his foul mood. "You're angry with me," she asserted evenly, hiding the depressed way the knowledge made her feel.

"No, not angry." Chaz dropped the corings in a pile at their feet. Straightening, he yanked off his glasses and let them dangle from one hand. Rubbing a hand across the sweat gathering on his jaw, he girded his thighs and rocked toward her slightly. "Exasperated, maybe."

Jenny looked into his eyes and thought she would drown, they were so blue. "Maybe?" she teased softly, trying to coax a laugh from him. "I'd say more like definitely."

Chaz shoved a hand through his hair, pushing the sun-streaked strands off his forehead. "If you'd let me drive, at the very least stayed on the road," he began.

"If I'd stayed on the road," Jenny interrupted archly, "we never would've seen that crater!"

The muscles in his chest grew even tighter against the formfitting fabric of his oversized navy shirt, but he merely pointed in the direction of the house, which was still a distance away, picked up the corings again and said, "Keep walking."

And walk they did, at a killer pace. Jenny struggled to keep up with his long, athletic strides. He had nearly run her into the ground when he finally shot her a sharp look. His glance narrowing even more, he said, "We'd better stop and rest."

"I don't need to rest."

Looking as impervious to the heat and humidity of the day as she was victim to it, he hissed out a short exhalation of breath and gave her a narrow-eyed glance. "Don't lie to me, Jenny. You're in no shape for this much activity, especially in this climate."

He was the one carrying the corings!

Jenny already felt embarrassed for driving the Jeep into the muck. She was not going to embarrass herself by wimping out on a simple walk back to the plantation house, too. "The hell I'm not in shape!" she countered emotionally.

Chaz regarded her skeptically.

"Feel my muscles," she demanded irately.

He stared down at her flushed pink cheeks and flashing sable eyes, unable to believe he'd heard right. "What?"

"I said feel my muscles!" Jenny raised the hem of her khaki walking shorts and looked him squarely in the eye. Smoothing her palm down the newly firm muscles of her thighs, over her knees, all the way to her calves, she said, "Feel them, Chaz! Feel how taut and strong they are!"

Chaz stared at her. Although there was nothing he would like better than to run his hands over her increasingly slender body, he didn't dare touch her. Not when he knew that would inevitably lead to something else. Something Jenny was very likely to regret once she got over the shock of Gary's affair with Lillian McCarry.

When he still didn't move, Jenny grabbed his palm and started to place it midway up her thigh. Only his hand and her skin never fully connected.

Instead, she found herself promptly backed up against the bark of a nearby tree. The next thing she knew his mouth was on hers. He was kissing her fiercely, with barely restrained passion, and she was kissing him back. His arms clamped around her waist and he lifted her against the erection straining the front of his jeans. The feel of him, so hard and demanding, was incredible. Like nothing she had ever felt. With a low moan, she wreathed her arms about his neck and melted willingly against him. When she was in his arms, she felt safe and protected, cherished and loved. Yes, she thought wistfully, bringing him even closer, as her tongue coaxed his into play, this is what I need. The only thing I need.

Just as suddenly as he had grabbed her, he drew away. Now what? Jenny wondered, dazed, as he released her abruptly, leaving her feeling cold and alone, and stalked away. He shoved both hands through his hair. In profile, he looked tough and dangerous, Jenny thought, much as he must have when he was a kid, growing up on the wrong side of the tracks.

His glance still averted, Chaz held up both hands in a gesture of surrender and grumbled, "Don't even say it, Jenny! I know I shouldn't have kissed you that way, but damn it." He whirled to face her and strode toward her, swiftly closing the distance between them. "You have to be careful. You can't come on to a guy that way and not expect something to happen." He jammed his hands on his lean hips. "You're lucky I have scruples. You're lucky that I am your and Gary's friend."

Sadly Jenny realized he had kissed her for one reason only. And it hadn't been because he loved her, either.

"Okay, consider your point made," she said, her low voice sounding just as gruff and irritable as his had. Shame heated her cheeks. "I ought to know better than to come on to you that way. And I do. But you've got to quit treating me like a wimp." Stalking away from him, she reported fiercely, "I've been anything but a wimp on this trip. The only time I acted the least bit squeamish is when I saw the alligator swimming behind our boat. I admit it,"

Jenny said openly and honestly as she paced back and forth. "I was scared. I not only jumped a mile, I threw myself into your lap." And how good that had felt, she thought, almost as good as your instructional kiss just now. "But as for the rest of the time—"

"You've been a real trooper," Chaz interrupted, his voice surprisingly gentle.

Jenny met his eyes and found they were filled with kindness. Stunned speechless, it took her a moment to find her voice again. "Thank you."

The silence strung out between them. Confronted with his goodness, she wanted to go to him and throw herself into his arms again. But she knew she couldn't. Not without losing his friendship altogether. And as painful as it was for her to be nothing more than his latest damsel in distress, she didn't want to give him up altogether. That would mean not seeing him again. And she had come to count on seeing him over the past week.

She inhaled a deep, shaky breath. "As for why I did what I just did," Jenny began, knowing what she was about to say wasn't quite true but would ease the tension between them, "I never meant to come on to you."

Didn't you, Jenny? her inner voice said. Didn't you want him to notice what sexy legs you had? Didn't you want him to notice that since this trip started you've lost at least five pounds? Didn't you want him to drag you into his arms and kiss you senseless?

The truth was, she had been flirting with him untenably in recent days, wearing clothes that were often impractical but enhanced her femininity to the hilt, trying hard to make him want her the way she wanted him, when all she had done in reality was end up proving to herself that he would never think of her as anything but his late friend's widow.

"I guess I'm just excited about getting back in shape again. And I let my enthusiasm get the best of me," Jenny finished awkwardly. Uncomfortably aware of her unslaked desire, and the probability it was likely to remain an unassuaged ache, Jenny said stiffly, "Anyway, I'm sorry. It won't happen again."

"Fine." Chaz's tone was brusque. Too brusque for comfort, Jenny decided as she watched him slide his aviator sunglasses back over his eyes.

"Forgive me?" she asked softly.

Chaz nodded deferentially, but his tone was cool and heartbreakingly impersonal as he replied, "Of course."

JENNY WASN'T the person who needed to be forgiven, Chaz thought as they continued their trudge in the hot steamy weather back to the house. He was the one who ought to be apologizing to her for losing control that way.

He didn't want her to look back on this trip and feel he'd taken advantage of her. He owed her and

Gary more than that. And yet, even though he knew
he and Jenny were all wrong for each other, that he
wasn't anywhere close to fitting her profile for the
Mr. Right in her life, he couldn't help but be drawn
deeper and deeper into her spell. The stronger she
got, the more he desired her. The more fragile she
got, the more he wanted to protect her. When she
sassed him, he sassed her right back. When
she looked at him, her sable eyes all warm and soft
and dreamy... he groaned silently.

It was getting tougher and tougher to keep his
hands off her. Tougher to remain aloof when all he
wanted to do was tell her every secret thought and
hope and fantasy he'd ever had in his life. He wanted
her to be his, the way she had been Gary's....

Marriage! Chaz thought, stunned. Was he thinking marriage? Maybe he was. Not that it would ever
happen, not in a million years. Jenny might be with
him now but once back in Dallas, once she no longer
needed him, she'd get all wrapped up in her society
teas and social causes. She wouldn't have time for
him anymore. She wouldn't have the need. She
wouldn't understand his own need to see as much of
the world as he could while he was still young enough
to explore it. He'd go back to seeing her infre-
quently, at best. Only this time it would be different, he realized as his heart twisted with pain. This
time he would realize he had fallen in love with her.
And never in a million years would she ever love a
pauper like him back.

As they headed for the kitchen, she grabbed a pitcher of iced tea and a glass and headed straight for the maps and charts of geological surveys she'd left spread out all over the kitchen table. He watched her settle down with them and knew he couldn't handle even one more wild-goose chase and guarantee his self-control would remain intact. It was time for them to stop pretending they were just casual acquaintances, instead of potential lovers tottering on the brink. It was time for them to go back to their normal lives.

He got a glass for himself, pulled up a chair and sat down catercorner from her. He drained his glass in a single gulp, wiped the moisture from his mouth with the back of his hand and set his glass down with a thud. As she glanced up, he steepled his hands together. "Listen, Jenny, I think it's time we talk about what'll happen if our worst fears are realized and these corings turn out to be as worthless as they appear at the moment."

Jenny studied him in stony silence. "Are you telling me I should give up, if that does turn out to be the case?" she asked, her voice brittle.

"Yes. I'm saying *if that's the case* then maybe it's time you cut your losses, sold the properties and were done with them."

She picked up her own glass and drank deeply from it, not bothering to mask her resentment of his advice. "No way," she said flatly.

Chaz resisted the urge to simply haul her into his arms and kiss some sense into her. "Not even if I personally help you find buyers for all your properties?" he asked coolly.

Jenny stood up and pushed her chair back with a scrape. "I don't want or need that kind of help from you, Chaz!" Jenny said, frustration oozing from her every pore.

Chaz stood, too. He was more aware now than ever just exactly how important her fortune—every penny of the ten-million dollar trust—was to her. "Then what do you want from me?" he demanded grimly. His hormones still simmering from their encounter on the grounds, he waited for her answer. As he looked at her, their eyes met and held. And suddenly, God help him, God help them both, he knew what she was about to say. "Jenny." He pushed the word out on a strangled moan.

If she had resented him before, for beginning to make love to her when she was feeling vulnerable, she'd despise him this time. Because this time, he knew, if he started, he wasn't going to stop. This time, there'd be no pretending it didn't happen, no turning back.

She moved around the edge of the table and took a step toward him. Her sable eyes glinted up at him with the same unshakable determination she used to fuel her recent adventures. "We can't go on denying this, Chaz," she said softly, firmly.

Precisely what he'd been trying to say. Early on, he'd thought it would be enough to make love to her. Now he knew that wasn't true. "I don't want to hurt you," he said gruffly. He didn't want to make a fool of himself over a Dallas golden girl who had already let him know in no uncertain terms, via her profile of her Mr. Right, that he wasn't the man for her.

She took another step closer. She tilted her head back to study his face. "You won't hurt me."

He couldn't hurt her. Not feeling the way he did about her. Okay, Jenny schooled herself reasonably, so maybe what he felt for her wasn't love. But there was tenderness and mutual concern. There was kindness between them. And understanding and fire, and a passion that put what Rhett and Scarlett had shared to shame.

She wanted Chaz as she had never wanted any man. During that kiss back on the grounds, she had finally accepted that. And having accepted the truth of the situation, she knew she had to take a risk, to act on that passion, just as she was acting on her need to set her estate to rights and regain her trust fund. So Chaz wouldn't marry her in the end, wouldn't give up his adventuring to be with her. So what? They could still have this time together. They could still have the adventure of being together, of sharing this incredible passion. She would have the memories of their time together for the rest of her life. If she backed away from this, if she didn't take advantage of the chance to be with him, she'd have the regret for the rest of her life.

Chaz looked down at her. He could see her mind working like a powerful computer. He could see that she had thought it out, and that later she wouldn't resent him for making love to her. Suddenly he could no more deny her than he could deny himself air. He swept her up into his arms and headed for the stairs. Jenny wreathed her arms about his neck. "Chaz, you don't have to carry me!" She laughed breathlessly, then cuddled even closer.

"I know but I want to," he said. He wanted this to feel like a honeymoon, to feel as special and preordained for her as it was for him.

Loving the feel of his warm, strong arms around her as much as she liked the unabashedly ardent light in his eyes, Jenny asked, "Where are you taking me?"

Chaz paused on the landing and shifted her in his arms. "You know where I'm taking you, Jenny," he said softly. *To that big four-poster bed she'd been sleeping in.*

Her eyes sparkled with anticipation. Enjoying the power she had over him, enjoying the desire swamping them both, she pressed a playful kiss below his ear and nibbled her way down his jaw. "Maybe I don't," she teased as her breath soughed out over his skin.

Chaz groaned. For a moment she thought he might drop her. Then his arms tightened around her.

He backed up against the wall and leaned against it. Still holding her tightly in his arms, he lowered his mouth to hers, kissed her slowly, lovingly. Fires raged inside her. Stunned at how quickly he could rouse the dormant woman inside her, Jenny sighed her need and kissed him back. "Beginning to get the idea?" Chaz rasped at length.

Jenny nodded. She still didn't know which room he had chosen for their tryst. She no longer cared. All that mattered was that finally, after days of confusion and unhappiness, the two of them were going to be together. Intimately, possessively together. She studied the primitive expression in his sea blue eyes and rubbed her thumb across his lower lip, which still glistened wetly from their kiss. She wanted him so much, she thought weakly, she didn't care if he took her right then and there. She bent and kissed him again, lightly this time. "Chaz?"

"Hmm?"

His voice sounded as dreamy and contented as she felt. As if he wanted fulfillment, but he wanted it to last forever. "Hurry," she said.

That one word was all the encouragement he needed. "Good thinking."

He strode up the stairs, his steps both purposeful and easy, then sauntered down the hall to her bedroom. He grinned again as they entered and Jenny knew why. It was a mess. Suitcases open. Clothes strewn here and there.

To her surprise, Chaz bypassed the poster bed in favor of the chaise that was next to the French doors. He laid her down on it. Looking up at the rapacious lines of his face, Jenny's pulse pounded. It seemed she never knew quite what to expect from him.

"Now what are you doing?" she demanded breathlessly, unable to understand why he hadn't chosen the bed. She propped herself up on both elbows as he stripped off his shirt, tossed it aside and knelt on the floor beside her.

Chaz smiled and reached for the first button on her blouse. He nuzzled a string of kisses down her neck, then whispered in her ear, "I'm undressing you." His lips trailed along her jaw and back to her throat. Her heart pounding, she felt his hands move nimbly down the row of buttons. When the cloth was parted, his gaze swept over her, taking in her translucent camisole top and the creamy white slopes of her breasts beneath. She sucked in her breath and moistened her dry lower lip with the tip of her tongue. "Wouldn't the bed be more comfortable?" she asked hoarsely as his fingers went to the ribbon tie on her eyelet lace camisole top.

Chaz inclined his head to their left, at the closed white sheers beneath the heavy blue velvet drapes. "I want to make love to you in the sunlight. See how it streams in through the windows, even when the sheers are closed?"

It did, Jenny thought. It illuminated the golden streaks in his chestnut hair, and bathed his bare back and chest in warm golden light. "But—"

"We'll get to the bed, Jenny," Chaz whispered, pushing her gently back, so she lay flat against the chaise. "I promise. Just not yet." He bent to kiss the uppermost curves of her breasts swelling over the sweetheart neckline of eyelet lace. He fastened his lips around one nipple and thoroughly kissed and laved the taut peak through the cloth, before moving to the other. Jenny shifted beneath him restlessly. He returned to her mouth where he kissed her with leisurely abandon, until she shuddered with delicious anticipation. "For now," he said softly, "I want you right here. Like this."

Need ribboned through her as he continued to stroke and caress her breasts. She breathed in the scent of him, her body begging for release. Jenny wrapped her arms around him and held him close. She kissed him slowly, deliberately. "Then that's what I want, too," she said.

His blue eyes dark with desire, he untied the bow and loosened the ribbon lacing on her chemise. Pushing the fabric aside, he gazed down at her lovingly. Her breasts were every bit as beautiful as he recalled. High and full. The nipples a taut, dark pink. Ruthlessly checking his own desire, he rubbed the nipples to demanding peaks, then bent and followed the upper curves with his mouth, tracing the fullness with his lips and then his tongue. As long as he lived, he thought, he would never get enough of the taste or feel of her. And though he might never be able to give her anything more than a love affair, he would make their lovemaking as perfect and satisfying for her as he knew how.

Sensations rippled through her, making her aware of all she had missed all her adult life. Lovemaking had never been like this. Never been so all-encompassing, so... thrilling.

Jenny tunneled her hands through his hair. "Oh, Chaz," she whispered as her back arched off the chaise, pressing her breast even deeper into his mouth.

Chaz sucked and caressed the eager peak. "Do you want me to stop?"

"No, don't," she moaned. Her hands clutched the silky warmth of his broad shoulders, and brought him closer still. He let his lips trail sensually beneath one breast, around to the center, then caressed the other in a lazy figure eight. She arched against him restlessly, her breath catching in her throat as his hand slid down to caress her inner thighs.

Stunned and touched by his selflessness, she pulled him up until his face was even with hers. "Come here," she murmured sexily against his mouth.

Chaz had never seen her look so sweet or so shy as she did at that second when she guided his mouth down to hers, yet her kiss was anything but shy— fiery and full of passion and a grown woman's need. Her tongue swept his mouth, mingled erotically with his. Blood pumped into his groin, making him harder still, but he kept his focus on Jenny, on the kiss, on making her feel everything she could possibly feel—first. Only then, only when he was sure she was fulfilled, would he satisfy his own need.

But Jenny, it seemed, had a mind of her own. Her fingers stroked the whorls of dark hair on his chest, tracing across his flat male nipples, and then down to his navel. The next thing he knew, she was guiding him down, so they were touching skin to skin. Chaz groaned as her nipples burrowed into his chest hair. She made soft, whimpering sounds in the back of her throat and shifted her hands across his back, clutching him to her, holding him tight.

Jenny reveled in the warmth of him, and the languid dizziness pouring through her. She had never guessed it could be like this, that kissing and petting could be an end to itself. Hungry for more, she moved against him, dragging her nipples across the soft thick pelt of his chest hair, rubbing against the hard musculature of his chest. Chaz murmured his satisfaction at her aggressiveness, then wrapped his arms about her, pulled her close and kissed her with a thoroughness that left her dizzy and aching for more.

"You feel so good," he murmured as she pressed a line of kisses down the strong, tanned column of his throat.

"So do you," Jenny said. She loved the delicious weight of him bearing down on her, the pressure of his arousal between her parted thighs, and the need that intensified inside her with every touch, every kiss. Wanting more, she slid her hands inside the waistband of his shorts.

The softness of her palms against the heat of his stomach almost undid him. He had wanted her for days now. He wasn't sure he could contain himself if she continued.

Putting aside his own needs momentarily, he reverently withdrew her palms. "Ladies first," he murmured as he unbuckled the belt at her waist, undid the button and brought the zipper down with a soft whoosh. Seconds later, her shorts were on the floor beside them. She blushed as he gazed at her flat abdomen and the delicate panties that barely covered the triangle of silky golden curls.

Burning to touch and taste all of her, Chaz started at her navel and kissed his way down, moving his lips over the silk. When he reached the groove at the apex of her thighs, she arched off the chaise. Determined to make this wonderful for her, he slipped his hands beneath her thighs and held her still. Hooking his thumbs beneath the elastic of her panties, he drew them down to midthigh. Her breath came in soft rapid pants as she gave herself up to him. She closed her eyes in silent surrender.

Aware what it was costing her to let her guard down so completely, to give herself over to abandonment, Chaz kissed the inside of both thighs, dipped his tongue in her navel and worked his way down to the dewy pink softness. She responded with an ecstatic cry. He deepened the caress, touching her intimately with his lips, fingertips and tongue.

"Oh, Chaz," she whispered brokenly, trembling, the tears of release streaming down her flushed cheeks.

"Feels good?"

"I want you inside me."

"Then you'll have it." His mouth fused to hers in a searing, sensual kiss, he lifted her hips and settled between her legs.

He was hot and hard against her. Jenny panicked, wondering if she'd be able to receive him, then realized as he shifted his weight to his forearms and pleasure rippled through her in deep, mesmerizing waves, that there was no need to be afraid of him. Not ever. Chaz knew exactly what to do. How to touch her, how to hold her, how to kiss her until the world narrowed to just the two of them. She'd never felt as consumed by passion as she did now. Never wanted a man more. And she did want him, Jenny thought as he slipped his hands beneath her and molded her hips to his. Wanted every part of him. Heart and soul.

"Jenny, my Jenny," Chaz whispered, then plunged deep inside her, slowly withdrew and plunged again. Waves of ecstasy rippled through her, as strong and pleasurably insistent as his kisses. Jenny's eyes closed. The pleasure, the passion, the sheer adventure of being with him, was so much more thrilling than she'd ever expected. And it was satisfying, too, in a very elemental, soulful way.

"Sweetheart, I don't want to rush you—" But he didn't know how much longer he could hold back.

Jenny dug her hands into the muscles of his back and wrapped her legs around his waist, savoring the sweet, blissful feel of him inside her. "You're not...rushing me," she said, her legs trembling against his as his weight crushed her down onto the chaise.

"How—?"

"Like that, Chaz. Yes. Nice and slow and... deep..."

"Like this?"

"Yes," Jenny whispered hoarsely, moaning as he went deeper still. "Yes."

Needing her as he'd never needed any woman, Chaz thrust inside her again, giving as much of himself to her as she could take. Her tight warmth closed around him like a velvet glove. He pushed deeper still, savoring the sweet intimacy of their joining. The blending of not just their wills, but of their hearts and minds and souls. This was not simply passion, he thought, plunging deeper still, but love. The love he had always wanted.

The completeness of his possession rocked her to her core. Jenny cried out, as did he, and then her entire world lit up, like the sky on the Fourth of July.

Tears of release slid down her face. But this time they were tears of love. This time, Jenny thought as her heart and mind filled to overflowing, this time there was no regret.

Chapter Thirteen

"What are you doing now?" Chaz asked, early the next morning. Pleasurably exhausted from their night of lovemaking, he was still in bed, but Jenny had been up since dawn. First showering, then calling Dufrene's Bait Shop to arrange for someone to get their rented Jeep out of the mud.

Jenny put down her cup of coffee and headed for the row of suitcases spread out over the floor. She bent as far as her skirt would allow and neatly folded in several days' worth of clothing. "I'm packing."

Chaz rolled onto his side and watched her stride across the room to retrieve a pair of heels. She slid them into a satin shoe bag and placed it on top of the neatly folded clothes. "Why?" He had hoped to stay there at least one more day, making love and discovering all they had yet to learn about each other.

Jenny straightened. In a two-piece sapphire blue suit that hugged her slender figure—tucking in at the waist, flouncing out in a seductive ruffle around her hips—she looked much as she usually did in Dallas. Rich, successful and very untouchable in that pampered, society-girl way.

Jenny spritzed herself with perfume, then ran a brush through her shiny golden hair. "I'm going to see Gary's mistress."

Chaz watched as she rummaged through her jewelry box. "Why?"

Jenny picked up a pair of hammered gold earrings. Pausing before the vanity mirror, she clipped one on each earlobe, then met his probing glance in the mirror. "If anyone knows why Gary purchased these properties," Jenny said almost too calmly for Chaz's taste, "she does."

His pulse pounding, Chaz sat up in bed. He rested his forearms on his bent knees. "Do you think that's wise?"

Jenny shrugged, then turned to face him. "It's funny," she said with quiet honesty and an easy smile. "I'm not jealous of her any longer. At least not in the all-consuming way I used to be."

Of course not, Chaz thought as he studied Jenny's excessive display of self-control. *Because you know now, from your all-night lovemaking session with me, that there's nothing wrong with you, nothing to make Gary run to another woman.* He had given her that. And that's all she had ever wanted from him, he realized sadly, just regained sexual self-esteem. He shook his head grimly, aware he'd been played a fool by a golden girl once again.

And yet, even knowing how Jenny had used him, whether inadvertently or deliberately, didn't change the way he felt about her, Chaz thought. He still wanted to protect and watch over her with every fiber of his being. And the protective side of him told him she was making a big mistake. "Do you think that's wise?" he asked her softly as she slipped on a necklace that matched her earrings.

"Expecting a cat fight?" Jenny teased. Then, unable to manage the catch on her necklace, she crossed to his side and sank down onto the bed, her back to him.

Chaz caught the intoxicating drift of her perfume as he fastened the clasp. "You're promising me there won't be one?"

Jenny's spine stiffened. She rose from the bed in one smooth, regal motion. "That all depends on what she says," she said carefully, meeting his eyes with a candid sable gaze. "I admit I could be moved to claw her eyes out."

Which means she still loves Gary, Chaz thought, depressed. "Hasn't Gary already hurt you enough?"

"Until I find out the why behind his actions, Chaz, I'll never have any peace."

Chaz got up and went into the bathroom that connected their two rooms. He spread a handful of shaving cream over his cheeks and chin and began to shave with short, careful strokes of the blade. "I can understand that. I'm curious, too. But that doesn't mean you have to do everything yourself, Jenny."

Especially something so potentially painful. "Let your lawyers handle it. After all, that's what you pay them for."

"I know that." Jenny leaned a shoulder against the doorframe. She watched as he finished, then rinsed his face. "However, I'd just as soon not have to explain Gary's personal treachery to them. I've been humiliated enough already."

Chaz patted his face dry. "Then let me handle it."

Jenny shook her head. "I couldn't ask you to do that."

Chaz stepped into the shower and turned on the spray. "Why not?" he asked, looking at her over the top of the glass shower door.

Jenny smiled and watched as he lathered shampoo into his hair. "Because you've already done so much for me already," she said, then slipped out of the bathroom, letting him know that, in her mind anyway, the subject was closed.

But Chaz couldn't let go of it that easily. What had he done for her, besides accompany her on this trip? And then there was their lovemaking. He knew the act of making love had somehow brought Jenny back to life again, heart and soul. But was that all it had done? he wondered suddenly as he briskly soaped himself from head to toe, then stepped under the shower to rinse off. Or had it done something else, too, something he hadn't considered until now. Had the act of making love with him not just aided Jenny in regaining her sexual self-esteem, but also helped her avenge Gary's infidelity? And what better way to get back at Gary, Chaz thought bitterly, than by making love with his best friend?

Feeling as if he'd been sucker-punched in the gut, Chaz turned off the shower. He wrapped a towel around his middle, dried off with another and strode back into Jenny's bedroom. Watching her finish the rest of her packing, he told himself he was wrong about her, he had to be. And yet as he watched her cool, collected movements, a nagging doubt remained. Had Jenny used him to get back at her late husband? Not deliberately...but inadvertently? Was that what her attraction to him had been all about?

Pushing the disturbing thought away, Chaz guided the conversation back to Jenny's current action plan. "Meeting Lillian McCarry could be ugly, Jen."

Jenny shrugged and snapped the latch shut on her suitcase. "Finding out about her was ugly."

Chaz ran a comb through his hair, slapped on some after-shave, then strode to her side. "You've already been hurt so much by Gary's infidelity." He hesitated, looking down into her sable eyes, and wished with all his heart he could make love to her again, that they could stay at the plantation one more day. "Can't you just let it go?" he asked quietly.

Jenny shook her head. Her chin thrust out stubbornly. "No, Chaz, I can't," Jenny said. Her soft, firm voice told him that it didn't matter how he felt or what he said, she wasn't going to change her mind or take his feelings into account. "I have to see this through to the bitter end, no matter how painful it is for me. Don't you understand?''

He was beginning to, Chaz thought grimly.

JENNY WAS glad Chaz had come with her to meet Lillian. The door was answered almost immediately by a pretty woman who Jenny guessed to be in her mid- to late-thirties. Jenny extended her hand graciously. "Ms. McCarry?''

"Yes.'' Lillian swept a hand through her sexily coiffed dark brown hair.

"I'm Jenny Olson. Gary Olson's wife.''

Lillian's light green eyes became even more guarded. "I know who you are.''

Jenny let her gaze drift over the woman's admittedly voluptuous hourglass figure, encased in tight jeans and an even more revealing emerald green sweater. "Then may I come in?''

Lillian cast a glance at Chaz, then at Jenny and lifted a careless hand. "Suit yourself.''

Jenny followed the other woman into a cozy, well-appointed living room. "You knew my husband,'' she began, trying her best to keep this on a business-like level.

"Yes,'' Lillian admitted freely, moving a stack of geological reports from the sofa so they could sit down. She walked over and flicked off her computer. "We caved together. I was with him when he died.''

Jenny swallowed hard. Her next question was going to be harder. She hated the prospect of being humiliated, especially in front of Chaz, and yet she knew for her own peace of mind that she had to know the truth, so she could deal with it and then go on with her life, so she could be free to love Chaz. "Only it wasn't an accident that the two of you were paired together, as you led everyone to believe, was it?" Jenny said.

Lillian's face paled.

"You were very close to Gary," Jenny continued, knowing from the other woman's guilty reaction that her hunch about this was right. "Close enough to spend time with him in Idaho, New Mexico, Colorado and Louisiana, as well."

Her jaw set angrily, Lillian got up to pace the room angrily. "What do you want?"

"The truth," Jenny said bluntly. She leaned forward urgently. "Why was Gary interested in those proprieties? And don't try to con me. I know you were there with him."

Lillian looked at Chaz, who was silent, then back at Jenny. Realizing they weren't going to leave until she'd confessed, Lillian finally sighed and said, "He was looking for places to develop. You know, places to put resorts."

Jenny wasn't sure why, but she knew the other woman was lying. "Why the geological reports then?"

Lillian's mouth gaped open in shock. "You know about those, too?"

"Yes, I do."

"I see," Lillian said slowly. "Well, we were looking for fault lines. We wanted to make sure nothing was in an earthquake zone."

More lies, Jenny thought. Chaz had been right. This was a waste of time. She rose abruptly. "This is pointless, Chaz. Let's go."

"Wait." Lillian McCarry put out a hand to delay their departure. "I'll—I'll buy the properties from you."

Jenny shook her head. "No deal."

"You can't want them for anything," Lillian protested emotionally.

"Sorry to disappoint you," Jenny bluffed, "but we do. You see, Chaz and I figured out why Gary thought those properties were so valuable. We found eight corings, Lillian. And knowing that, there's no way on earth we'd sell."

Lillian's expression grew even more stormy. "You can't rip me off. I won't let you. I have signed agreements, giving me half the mineral rights on all of those properties."

"Why would Gary do something like that?" Chaz asked.

"Because it was my idea Gary purchase them," Lillian shot back hotly. "I went to him, looking for an investor to help me purchase the properties, which by the way are worth millions, or they will be, once the deposits of platinum and palladium are announced."

Jenny sucked in a shocked breath but outwardly managed to keep her cool. "Why didn't Gary tell me any of this?" she demanded.

Lillian slipped her hands into the pockets of her jeans. "He wanted to surprise you. It's true," she continued at their skeptical expressions. "He always felt a little uneasy about his blue-blooded-but-broke background, the fact that when you married, the two of you had lived on your trust fund as well as his earnings. He wanted to bring wealth to your marriage, too, Jenny. He planned to surprise you when the deed was done."

"And the caving?"

"We had reason to believe, from some initial studies, that palladium and platinum were there, too, but that proved false. I'm sorry," Lillian said, sadness flickering in her light green eyes. "I never wanted anything to happen to him."

Nor had she, Jenny thought. But it had. And his treachery had inevitably ended their marriage. "You shouldn't have slept with him," she told Lillian.

"I didn't." Lillian looked at her in surprise. "He was in love with you, Jenny. Only you."

"Do you believe her?" Chaz asked as they returned to their rental car. Looking quiet, almost withdrawn, Jenny slipped into the passenger seat. He climbed behind the wheel.

"Yes," Jenny said slowly as she put on her shoulder belt, "corny as it sounds, I do." She turned to him, her sable eyes wide, vulnerable. "Is that only ego talking? Am I foolish for wanting to believe she didn't sleep with Gary?"

"I don't know." Chaz shrugged. "But looking into her eyes, recalling the Gary we both knew, I believed her, too. It made sense." *The next question is,* Chaz thought, *are you sorry you slept with me, Jenny? Now that you know Gary wasn't unfaithful to you, are you sorry we made love?*

Chaz started the car and headed in the direction of the Atlanta airport, for their return trip to Dallas. "At least now I don't have to worry about my trust fund." Jenny sighed.

"You'll get all the money Gary invested, and more. Much more." He gave her a sidelong glance. Eyes closed, she was resting her head against the back of the seat. Though it had been a long day, she still looked as pretty, and untouchable, as she had that morning. "You must feel relieved," he said.

Jenny pushed out a breath. She lifted her head and stared out the windshield at the rush hour traffic ahead of them. "I do and I don't," she admitted. "Mostly, I'm just tired." She turned to him, her eyes soft, beseeching. "I know I promised you dinner when we returned to Dallas, but do you mind if I beg off?"

Chaz concealed his hurt. "Of course not."

"Maybe we can do it some other time," Jenny suggested.

His heart aching, Chaz nodded.

"It's nothing you've done or said. Really. You've been wonderful," Jenny continued, evidently realizing his feelings were hurt. "It's just me. So much has happened. I—I feel I have to be alone tonight."

Like I don't know when I'm getting the brush-off, Chaz thought. What had he expected? That now that they'd made love she would forget everything? That she would forget the golden cocoon in which she'd been brought up? Not damn likely, he thought as his hands tightened over the steering wheel of the rental car.

No, the truth was, he had made love to her and it had been as exciting and wonderful and gratifying an experience as either of them could have wished. But that was because she'd gotten sex mixed up with her excitement over having her first real-life adventure. Now that they were going back home again to familiar circumstances, now that Jenny had taken firm control of her life once again, her problems solved, their adventure finished, their brief love affair was over, too. She just didn't know how to tell him that.

Fighting his own feelings of jealousy and inadequacy, but wanting Jenny to be happy, Chaz signaled his intention to turn left ahead, and said, "Before we left, you remember what you asked me?"

"What?" Jenny looked at him blankly.

Chaz directed the car onto the airport exit. "About introducing you to suitable beaux. Do you still want me to do that?" he asked, as graciously as he was able. Jenny would see she wasn't the only one who could conduct herself with old-money charm and gentility.

Jenny blinked. Just as quickly, her expression became closed and unreadable. "Sure, why not," Jenny said. "And anyway, now that we're going home," she reflected, then paused to briefly rake her teeth across her delectable bow-shaped lower lip, "it will probably be more important than ever."

Chaz regretted the change of the traffic light that forced him to tear his eyes from Jenny's face and drive on. "Why do you say that?" he asked as he pulled into the airport and hunted for the signs to the rental car office.

Jenny shrugged insouciantly, as if her dating someone else were of absolutely no significance. "Because. I've solved all my problems," she said matter-of-factly. She looked away from him, refusing to meet his eyes. "I don't expect you to keep hovering over me. I'm fine. Your..." Her voice caught slightly before she could go on in a deliberately cool, steel-magnolia voice. "Your job is finished."

"You're sure that's what you want?" Chaz asked as he guided the car to a stop in front of the Hertz sign, wishing his own mood weren't so grim, her words so final.

Jenny nodded. And in that instant, he thought, she had never seemed more sure of herself. "Absolutely. Fix me up, Chaz," she said, pushing from the car. "The sooner the better."

"HEY, CHAZ, is it true, what they said in the paper about that friend of yours being a multi-multi-millionaire?"

Chaz looked at his newest employee, Tommy Burke, who at seventeen reminded him so much of himself. The kid was smart as a whip, yet he wore the chip on his shoulder he'd earned for growing up on the wrong side of the tracks as proudly as any badge. He'd been in and out of trouble since he could walk. Only Chaz's promise to the judge, to personally keep an eye on Tommy, give him a job and keep him out of trouble, had kept him out of the juvenile detention center. "Yep. Jenny Olson signed a deal with United Minerals, Inc. to mine the platinum and palladium on her properties."

"Gee, that makes her one rich lady," Tommy said, looking for a moment like a young James Dean, with his swept-back hair and T-shirt sleeves rolled up to expose his biceps.

"Her money isn't the most important thing about her, Tommy," Chaz said gruffly. He would've loved Jenny the same, rich or poor.

"I know that," Tommy hastened to add as he took a stack of towels out of the dryer and began folding them.

Yes, but did Jenny?

"Well, you don't have to look so grim. The two of you are still friends, aren't you?" Tommy persisted.

"Platonic," Chaz allowed.

"Oh. I get it. In your place, I'd be sad, too. Just kidding!" Tommy grinned and held up both hands in a gesture of surrender. He resumed folding the towels. "If you feel that way about her, how come you don't go after her?"

Because my business with Jenny is over. She made that perfectly clear when she sent her accountant over with the eighty-thousand-dollar loan on the new gym. And if I hadn't gotten the message, there was no way in hell I could miss the import of her date with a prospective Mr. Right tonight.

Chaz picked up the clipboard and studied the proposed publicity schedule for the opening of his new gym. Frowning, he said, "There are some things you learn in this life. One of the first things is that oil and water don't mix."

Tommy grinned, looking as ready to argue with Chaz as ever. "They do if you shake them up real hard, in a bottle or something. Like salad dressing."

Chaz felt himself tense even more. It had been hard enough telling himself it was over, without having to make someone else believe it, too. "But just like salad dressing," Chaz explained, schooling his new employee, "as soon as you set the bottle down, as soon as you let things return to normal, the oil and the water separate again." Which meant

Jenny went back to her old way of life and her old friends, and he went back to his.

"Not always," Tommy disagreed. Finished folding the dry towels, he added another load of wet ones to the dryer. "Haven't you been in the grocery store aisles lately? They got a new kind, one that stays mixed all the time. I don't know how they do it. But it stays the way it should. Probably some magic ingredient."

Like love, Chaz thought, then chided himself for the unusually romantic thought.

"And anyway, what does salad dressing have to do with the way you're lusting unrequitedly after your lady friend?"

Chaz watched Tommy tear off a fabric softener sheet and toss it into the dryer. "Unrequitedly?"

"I know some big words." Tommy grinned as he turned the dryer on with a quick slap of his hand. "I just don't use them all the time."

"Well, you should," Chaz said, reaching for his jacket. Tommy made more sense than he knew. At least he hoped that was the case, that he wasn't doing something Jennyesque and going off half-cocked. "They make you sound wise," Chaz said.

Tommy blinked as Chaz strode past, his mind made up. "Hey, Chaz, where you going in such a hurry, man? Where you going?"

"I'M SORRY." Jenny struggled to concentrate on what her handsome and sophisticated date was saying. "You were saying?"

Rex stiffened his shoulders beneath his Yves Saint Laurent suit. "Normally, I don't mind repeating myself, but in this case I'm not sure it matters."

Jenny flushed, embarrassed. She hadn't meant to be rude. "I really am sorry."

"And you really are disinterested."

"I didn't say that!" Jenny protested, feeling very guilty. She knew how much trouble Chaz had gone to fix her up on this date.

"No," Rex agreed drolly, "you just show it every time your eyes glaze over."

Jenny took a deep breath. She couldn't continue on this way. She had to make something work out right! Heaven knows she had screwed up her relationship with Chaz. If it had even been a relationship, she thought. More and more, it seemed like some wild, crazy, utterly romantic, utterly unrealistic dream. One she wasn't over yet. Maybe because for the first and only time in her life, she'd felt loved as herself. Chaz had known she was broke, but he had still stayed with her, still made love to her as if there was no tomorrow. Her losing her trust fund really hadn't mattered to him. But, Jenny thought, she had the feeling it would matter very much to someone like Rex if she no longer had the money to buy the right clothes, or live in the right house, in the right neighborhood.

Forcing herself to concentrate, Jenny met Rex's eyes and apologized for her lack of attentiveness. "I'm sorry. I really am. Let's start from the beginning. You tell me about this building that you're designing and I'll really try to understand."

"Okay. It's a high rise, in the downtown district of Fort Worth..."

Jenny attempted to listen intently, thinking that in the dim restaurant lighting, Rex looked even more handsome than he had when he'd picked her up. But all Jenny could think about these days, no matter where she was or what she was doing, was Chaz. And how Chaz had looked the night they'd gone out to dinner, shortly after her thirtieth birthday. It had been weeks, but she could still recall exactly what he'd worn. The rumpled blue cotton shirt and khaki slacks, the restaurant blazer. Just as she could remember how he looked when he'd shown up at the children's hospital, to take her on that killer walk.

The truth was, it didn't matter how he dressed or what he said or even what he was doing. When Chaz was in a room, she felt as if she had a giant magnet attached to her heart, propelling her to him. When Chaz was in the room, she couldn't stay away, couldn't keep from goading him into kissing her, or kissing him back, couldn't keep herself from doing anything and everything to get and keep his attention. Even if it meant wearing a gauzy white, hopelessly feminine, and incredibly sexy white tea dress in a Louisiana swamp!

"You see," Rex crowed, "there you go again. I start talking and your eyes glaze over. I might as well be on another planet."

Flushing guiltily, Jenny said, "Maybe we should try dancing."

"Maybe." Rex got up gruffly and led her onto the dance floor. "You know, you're a pretty woman, Jenny Olson. A very wealthy woman. But I'm only doing this as a favor to Chaz."

Jenny clasped his hand in hers and wished it were Chaz's. "I know."

Rex tilted his head to the side, perplexed. "You know?"

"Of course," Jenny said, wondering all the while how Chaz would dance. Heaven knows he did everything else with supreme physical grace. "I asked him to fix me up with someone," she explained.

"If that's truly the case...you know, Jenny, it might help if you looked like you were the least bit interested," Rex suggested helpfully. "Or is it me?"

"It's not you." Jenny shook her head, dismissing that idea. "It's me, Rex."

"You?" Rex echoed, confused.

"Yes. I'm—" She hesitated, then thought, why the hell not, she was never going to see this man again anyway. "I'm in love with someone else."

"Oh," Rex said heavily. He nodded as if this explained everything. "Does Chaz know?" he asked sympathetically.

Considering the passionate way they'd made love, it would be hard for him not to know, she thought. "I'm afraid so," she admitted sadly.

"And?" Rex prodded.

Jenny shrugged. "And it's why he agreed to fix me up, I guess." *Because he wanted to get rid of me.*

"Because the love is unrequited?" Rex guessed.

Jenny nodded sadly. "Yes."

"I'm sorry, Jenny."

"So am I," she said, marveling that dancing to such soft, sexy music in the incredibly plush surroundings could be such an unromantic activity. *You'll never know how sorry I am. Chaz will never know how sorry I am.*

Rex pulled her nearer. "Listen, Jenny," he whispered softly in her ear. "If it'll make you feel any better, I'll—"

"All right buddy, that's close enough!" a rude and rough male voice interrupted. Jenny's heart took a soaring leap.

"Chaz!" Jenny and Rex said in mutual astonishment. What was he doing there? Jenny wondered.

"That's right," Chaz responded grimly. "And from the looks of things, it's a good thing I arrived when I did, too."

Not sure what she was being accused of, only knowing she didn't like it, Jenny rolled her eyes. How like the man to brush her off one minute, then try to lay claim to her the next. Well, if Chaz thought he could take her for granted he had another think coming. Her mouth set with a mixture of anger and exasperation, Jenny averted her glance from his probing blue eyes and complained, "I can't believe you are actually childish enough to show up here and ruin the date you arranged, Chaz!" Not to mention embarrass her in a place where they were both well-known.

"Yeah, Chaz," Rex interrupted. "Jenny and I were just getting close." Chaz gave him a look. "Or maybe we weren't," Rex mumbled.

Rex tried to let her go. Jenny held on tight, as around them a wide swath cleared. Dancers stopped to watch the unexpected floor show.

"After all," Jenny continued hotly, as all the emotions she'd been holding so tightly in check surged to the fore. The man had abandoned her without a second thought, for heaven's sake, and then in his haste to get rid of her, had actually tried to foist her off on someone else. The fact that his matchmaking effort had been prearranged, Jenny assured herself emotionally, was beside the point. "It's not as if you have anything better to offer me, Chaz!" she said, and had the satisfaction of seeing his mouth tighten into a thin white line. "Like love!"

"Wait a minute!" Chaz interrupted, shoving Rex aside and taking her into his arms. "You think I don't love you?"

Hot, angry color flooded her face. Jenny jammed her hands on her hips. "What am I supposed to think, after the way you dumped me?"

"Dumped you!" Chaz echoed, incensed. "I never dumped you."

"No," Jenny agreed, making no effort to hide the irony in her low voice, "you just foisted me off on an unsuspecting client from your gym."

"Rex is exactly like you!" Chaz protested.

"Now I take exception to that!" Jenny shot back hotly.

"You know what I mean," Chaz corrected. "Rich."

Jenny let out an exasperated breath. "Like I care a hoot what Rex was born with!" Jenny sputtered.

Chaz pushed a hand through the tousled layers of his chestnut hair. He was the only man in the elegant restaurant not in a coat and tie, and yet Chaz outshone all of them, even dressed in khaki trousers and a rumpled light blue oxford cloth shirt. "Okay, if not money, or breeding, then what do you care about?" Chaz demanded.

Jenny lifted her chin another challenging notch. She damned the man for breaking her heart, and herself for loving him anyway. "If you had half the sense you were born with, Chaz Lovgren," she stormed, "you'd know!"

Temper brought a rush of color into his ruggedly handsome face. "Well, I don't!" he volleyed back heatedly. "I don't have the foggiest notion of what you're talking about!"

Afraid if she stood there one second longer she would lose her resolve never to be hurt by another man again, Jenny sent him a haughty glance, then pivoted on her heel and strode in the other direction. "You wouldn't," she said, over her shoulder.

"Don't walk away from me."

Jenny spun around to face him. Ignoring his annoyed look, she said, "There's only one thing you can say that will stop me, Chaz Lovgren. Only one word."

"I don't know about words," Chaz said hoarsely as he closed the distance between them abruptly. At the raw note of emotion in his voice, she lifted her face and met his eyes. "I only know one thing. I'm miserable without you," he whispered, taking her into his arms and holding her close.

Jenny was miserable without him, too. But without that one thing, without that one magical ingredient, it would never work, she knew. "And that's it?" She blinked back tears.

Chaz shrugged, his broad shoulders straining the fabric of his shirt.

She waited and then realized with numbing disappointment that he wasn't going to say it. Probably didn't even feel it. Shoulders hunched forward, she started to push away from him once again.

This time, he didn't let her go but held tight. "Jenny, I love you," Chaz said softly. "Please, you've got to give me another chance. You've got to give us another chance."

Her heart doing cartwheels in her chest, Jenny blinked. "What did you say?"

"I said I love you!" Chaz repeated, knowing he was about to make a fool of himself in front of a whole roomful of people, but no longer caring. If Jenny didn't give him another chance, what did it matter?

Without her, he had finally figured out, he didn't have much of a life.

Tunneling his hands through her hair, he tilted her head back to his and whispered the words that had been in his heart for days. "For richer, for poorer. For better, for worse. I love you. I love you. I love you." He shook his head in bemusement at his own vulnerability where she was concerned. "I don't even care anymore if you don't love me back," he whispered tenderly, searching her sable eyes for any hint of returned affection. "How's that for putting it all on the line?"

"What do you mean you don't care if I don't love you back? Chaz, of course I love you!" Jenny cried as tears of joy streamed down her face. "I've loved you for weeks now!"

He stared at her, hardly daring to believe it was true. "Cross your heart?" he asked hoarsely, the misery he'd felt ever since they left Atlanta finally fading.

"And hope to live with you forever and ever," Jenny confirmed. Standing on tiptoe, she sealed her vow with a kiss that was tender and giving and full of need. Chaz hauled her nearer and returned the kiss with searing velocity.

Jenny had no idea how much time passed before the hot, yearning caress ended, only that she was weak and shaking, and around them, the crowd of amused diners was clapping wholeheartedly.

"Well," Rex said dryly to one and all as he jabbed a thumb at his chest, "guess that means I'm out of the picture."

"I guess you are," Chaz said with a grin.

"Rex, I'm sorry," Jenny said, hating the thought that she'd made him uncomfortable.

"Don't be." Rex smiled at them both. "It's worth it to see two people so happy and obviously in love."

Jenny turned back to Chaz, relishing the warmth and strength of his arms. She had never been happier or felt more content than she did at that moment. "We are in love, aren't we?" she asked softly, feeling happier than she ever had in her life.

"Passionately, it would seem," Chaz affirmed, then held her close. He kissed her again, tenderly this time. "As long as I live, Jenny, you're going to be the only woman for me."

"Well, that makes two of us," she admitted with an emotional laugh, staring up at the face she loved so well, "because I know you're one of a kind."

"Marry me." It was more a command than a question.

"Yes," Jenny replied fiercely, hugging him close. "Oh, yes," she said. Joy flowed through her in wave after majestic wave.

"Right away?"

Jenny drew back to look at him. She could feel herself glowing from head to toe, and knew she didn't want to wait one second longer for the two of them to be together. The newly discovered adventurous side of her nature knew exactly how to accomplish their goal. "I hear they have all-night chapels in Vegas. And perfect honeymoon hotels. One of which I still happen to own."

Chaz grinned, recalling their last stay there. "With jungle themes?" he whispered wickedly in her ear.

Jenny laughed, the adventurous side of her imagining what it would be like to make love with Chaz in that water bed, with the mirrored ceiling overhead. It might seem strange to some that they'd elect to marry in such a wild and crazy place. But not to her. She knew it didn't matter where they tied the knot or spent their first night of wedded bliss. They would love each other forever. "I even know the manager—who might be persuaded to cut us a special deal. So, what do you say?" she teased, her eyes serious. "Shall we leave right away?"

"Only if you agree to go with me to Hawaii after that, and do some serious honeymooning," Chaz said, his eyes shining with love. "Say for two or three weeks?"

Jenny imagined making love with him in an island paradise and knew nothing could be more perfect. At last, it seemed, all her dreams were coming true. "Life with you is going to be a constant adventure, isn't it?"

Chaz grinned, confirming her every fantasy with one very sexy smile. "I'll show you the world, Jenny," he whispered softly.

Jenny held his eyes, knowing there was nothing she'd love more. She linked hands with him. "And I'll go, gladly." No more would she sit home alone, while the man in her life was off adventuring. This time around was going to be different. This time around she was going to see the whole world, too.

"Now, how about that honeymoon?" Chaz said as he bent to kiss her gently once again.

Safe in the knowledge that they were really going to be together, not just for today, but forever, Jenny returned his kiss, smiled and said, "Just let me get my running shoes and I'll race you to the plane."

HARLEQUIN®
A M E R I C A N ◆ R O M A N C E®

You asked for it...and now you've got it. More MEN!

MORE THAN MEN

We're thrilled to bring you another special edition of the popular MORE THAN MEN series.

Like those who have come before him, Sean Seaward is more than tall, dark and handsome. All of these men have extraordinary powers that make them "more than men." But whether they are able to grant you three wishes or to live forever, make no mistake—their greatest, most extraordinary power is that of seduction.

So make a date next month with Sean Seaward in
#538 KISSED BY THE SEA
by Rebecca Flanders

Take 4 bestselling love stories FREE

Plus get a FREE surprise gift!

Special Limited-time Offer

Mail to Harlequin Reader Service®

> 3010 Walden Avenue
> P.O. Box 1867
> Buffalo, N.Y. 14269-1867

YES! Please send me 4 free Harlequin American Romance® novels and my free surprise gift. Then send me 4 brand-new novels every month, which I will receive months before they appear in bookstores. Bill me at the low price of $2.89 each plus 25¢ delivery and applicable sales tax, if any.* That's the complete price and—compared to the cover prices of $3.50 each—quite a bargain! I understand that accepting the books and gift places me under no obligation ever to buy any books. I can always return a shipment and cancel at any time. Even if I never buy another book from Harlequin, the 4 free books and the surprise gift are mine to keep forever.

154 BPA ANRL

Name   (PLEASE PRINT)

Address   Apt. No.

City   State   Zip

This offer is limited to one order per household and not valid to present Harlequin American Romance® subscribers. *Terms and prices are subject to change without notice. Sales tax applicable in N.Y.

UAM-94R   ©1990 Harlequin Enterprises Limited

HARLEQUIN®
AMERICAN ◆ ROMANCE®

Once in a while, there's a man so special, a story so
different, that your pulse races, your blood rushes.
We call this

AMERICAN
ROMANCE®
heart
beat

Jason Hill is one such man, and HEAVEN KNOWS is one such book.

To Sabrina, Jason was so special that not even death could take him away. She could still hear
his laughter, see his beautiful face and feel his eyes on her. Was she mad...or was her husband still with her in their marriage bed?

HEAVEN KNOWS
by
TRACY HUGHES

Don't miss this exceptional, sexy hero. He'll make your HEARTBEAT!

Available in July wherever Harlequin books are sold.

Watch for more Heartbeat stories, coming your way soon!

HARLEQUIN®

Weddings, Inc.

EXPECTATIONS
Shannon Waverly

Eternity, Massachusetts, is a town with something special going for it. According to legend, those who marry in Eternity's chapel are destined for a lifetime of happiness. As long as the legend holds true, couples will continue to flock here to marry and local businesses will thrive.

Unfortunately for the town, Marion and Geoffrey Kent are about to prove the legend wrong!

EXPECTATIONS, available in July from Harlequin Romance®, is the second book in Harlequin's new cross-line series, **WEDDINGS, INC.** Be sure to look for the third book, **WEDDING SONG,** by Vicki Lewis Thompson (Harlequin Temptation® #502), coming in August.

American Romance is goin' to the chapel...with three soon–to–be–wed couples. Only thing is, saying "I do" is the farthest thing from their minds!

You're cordially invited to join us for three months of veils and vows. Don't miss any of the nuptials in

HARLEQUIN®

A M E R I C A N ◆ R O M A N C E ®

A NEW STAR COMES OUT TO SHINE....

American Romance continues to search the heavens for the best new talent... the best new stories.

Join us next month when a new star appears in the American Romance constellation:

Rosemary Grace
#544 HONKY TONK DREAMS
July 1994

Sam Triver had heard of unusual ways to meet a woman, but never this unusual. When he walked into the newsroom, there stood transplanted Texan Lonnie "Lone Star" Stockton—her six-guns pointed to the ceiling. It may not have been love at first sight—but you couldn't deny that sparks were flying!

RISING STAR

Be sure to Catch a "Rising Star"!

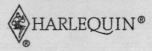

HARLEQUIN®

COMING SOON TO
A STORE NEAR YOU…

CHANCE
OF A LIFETIME

By *New York Times* Bestselling Author

This July, look for CHANCE OF A LIFETIME
by popular author
JAYNE ANN KRENTZ.

After Abraham Chance had wrongly implicated her sister in
an embezzlement scam, Rachel Wilder decided to do her
own sleuthing, posing as his housekeeper. Not only was
Chance onto her deception, he was uncovering a
passion in her even more consuming
than revenge.…

Watch for CHANCE OF A LIFETIME, available in July
wherever Harlequin books are sold.

JAK-CL